THE PROMISE OF LOVE

A BILLIONAIRE ROMANCE

SCARLETT KING

HOT AND STEAMY ROMANCE

CONTENTS

Sign Up to Receive Free Books   v
Blurb   vii

1. Chapter One   1
2. Chapter Two   8
3. Chapter Three   24
4. Chapter Four   38
5. Chapter Five   45
6. Chapter Six   50
7. Chapter Seven   61
8. Chapter Eight   65
9. Chapter Nine   73
10. Chapter Ten   79
11. Chapter Eleven   89
12. Chapter Twelve   98
13. Chapter Thirteen   109
14. Chapter Fourteen   119
15. Chapter Fifteen   129
16. Chapter Sixteen   135
17. Chapter Seventeen   143
18. Chapter Eighteen   149
19. Chapter Nineteen   161
20. Chapter Twenty   170
21. Chapter Twenty-One   177

    Sign Up to Receive Free Books   181
    Preview of The Dirty Doctor's Touch   183
    Chapter 1   185
    Chapter 2   190
    Chapter 3   195
    Chapter 4   200

Other Books By This Author   205
Copyright   207

Made in "The United States by:

Scarlett King

© Copyright 2020 – Scarlett King

ISBN: 978-1-64808-093-7

ALL RIGHTS RESERVED. No part of this publication may be reproduced or transmitted in any form whatsoever, electronic, or mechanical, including photocopying, recording, or by any informational storage or retrieval system without express written, dated and signed permission from the author

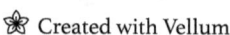 Created with Vellum

SIGN UP TO RECEIVE FREE BOOKS

Sign Up to Receive Free E-Books and Audiobook Codes.

Would you like to read **The Unexpected Nanny, Dirty Little Virgin** and **other romance books** for **free**?

You can sign up to receive these free e-books and audiobooks by typing this link into your browser:

https://www.steamyromance.info/free-books-and-audiobooks-hot-and-steamy/

Or this one:

https://www.steamyromance.info/the-unexpected-nanny-free/

BLURB

Ben Donovan owns a large corporation, and he is also known as a philanthropist for all his good deeds around the world. A scandal breaks out when his company is associated with an oil leak in the ocean. His team is on damage control, and they have to fix his reputation. His right-hand man suggests that he go to Africa to help build a school—it's a good PR move.
When he arrives in Africa, Ben comes across do-gooder Katie Bennett. The two have an instant connection, but when Katie finds out how Ben's been trying to cover up the oil leak back home, she questions everything she's learned about him. He tries to explain himself, but she shuts him down and ends up leaving Africa. Ben knows they have something special, but when he tries to win her back, he just might be too late.

I knew he was in the room before I entered it.
His gaze was that intense.
I tried to ignore it, but there he was.
He consumed my every thought.
I knew what I wanted though and I would not be played.
Come to me Ben, claim me as your own.

I needed him...
Ben Henricks knew how to touch me; I was powerless under his touch.
Can I risk everything, my heart for him?

His hands did pleasing things to my body.
I needed his touch.
My first orgasm came from his rough touch.
I couldn't help but moan when he touched me.
I ached for him, his touch, his mouth.
It broke me when I left him.
He was all I ever thought about.
Could I live without him? I wasn't sure...
When he touched me, I couldn't say no.

CHAPTER ONE

Ben

I sat at the head of the boardroom table, disgusted as I glanced around the room. I couldn't believe what had happened to my own company in such a short amount of time. What was the matter with the people I employed? How could such a disaster go unnoticed until it practically blew up in our faces—and in the news of all places? It was enough to make me blow my top, and I did just that.

"Shut up, all of you! I'm sick of listening to this blathering mess. Why don't you tell me who's responsible for this disaster!"

All heads turned to me in alarm. They were terrified of me, and they had every reason to be. I may be a young billionaire, but I ran a tight ship and I wasn't about to have anyone employed by me running around creating scandals at my company. I got to the top for a reason; I was damn smart.

There was silence all around the room. I looked at each and every one of my advisors and saw their fear reflected back to me.

A bunch of cowards, that's all they were. My company's reputation was being dragged through the mud, and they had nothing to say about the matter.

"I'm waiting."

They all stared at me in awe. They knew darn well that I wasn't the kind of boss that anyone messed with, and I knew they were all wondering if they would be fired that day. I might have to just let them all go and start with a fresh team the next day; I was that fed up with them. I needed the best people on my team, and they had fallen short lately. I wasn't sure how I was going to handle the situation, but I had to figure out a way to get my company out of the mess it was in before it was destroyed forever.

The company had recently been charged with criminal and —my god—federal charges for dumping industrial waste into the Arctic Ocean. The Arctic Ocean! Just thinking about that mess brought a rage in me that was barely contained. What was worse was that I had no idea these practices were going on behind my back. That was some moron's solution to getting rid of company waste: to pollute an ocean instead. It sickened me just thinking about it. I had to admit I was angrier at myself than at anyone else. I wasn't sure how something so massive could possibly get past me. How had I not known what was going on behind the scenes? Maybe I had been playing a little too much in life and not spending enough time getting dirty at my own company. That had to be it, right? I just wasn't paying attention, and now the company—*my* company—was paying the price.

I looked around the room again, trying to summon up some clarity on the whole situation. Could that be found?

"Imagine my surprise, ladies and gentlemen, when I return from a lovely vacation only to find out from my lawyers that I have a meeting with the prosecutor's office. When I get there, I find out that the company I have built from the ground up, my life's work, is being charged with a crime that is unfathomable to me. The company is supposed to be humanitarian, you buffoons, and yet we are filling the ocean with garbage? That's what I heard."

I was yelling now, and I could tell that my message would be heard in my employees' nightmares for weeks. My face was beet red, and yet I didn't care. I couldn't believe what had happened all while I was on vacation enjoying champagne and women. It was too terrible to even consider. I needed a moment to compose myself before I lost my mind completely. I needed a moment to assess their worth and see if they were even worthy of continuing their employment with me.

"I need to know who did this. I pray to god it's not one of my right-hand men or women here. I would hate to think it was my very own front-runners who thought this was appropriate behavior for the company. I have one hell of a mess to clean up here. I expect you to submit reports on the hour about how you all think we should make this situation right. I want further suggestions on where the waste should go from this day forward since we now know that the ocean isn't quite the place to dump it." My voice dripped with sarcasm as I glared at my team. "Now get out of my sight."

They hurried off and out of the office as quickly as they could. I watched my team filter out of the room, hoping that my point had been made. The only other man left in the room with me was my right-hand man, Kyle, the CEO.

I stared at him a moment and he stared back, meeting my gaze unwaveringly. He had to have known something like this was going on—how could he not? But then again, I owned the whole thing, and yet I didn't know. But wasn't it his job to know the ins and outs of the company while I was away playing? That was what he was hired for after all, though I didn't think he would ever betray me in that way.

"Kyle, please tell me you had nothing to do with this. Tell me you didn't know it was happening."

Kyle was one tough son of a bitch. I had only known him to be loyal in the many years he'd worked for me. It was hard to fathom he would do something so unbelievably stupid and immoral.

"Ben, I'm shocked that you even have to ask me such a thing. We've been a team for quite some time. I assure you that I had nothing to do with this. I'm as shocked as you are about the whole thing. It's surely a minion that pulled something like that, and I promise you we'll find out who did it. That person will be punished."

"I've always appreciated your loyalty, Kyle. You've been a great asset to me as well as the company for some time. But how is it that the CEO, the guy who is supposed to have my back when I'm away, how is it that you don't know something so substantial was being done? It's madness to me that industrial waste could be dumped into the ocean and no one in the higher division has an explanation for it."

"Ben, it wasn't me. There are other people in charge of saving the company money, and this was obviously a decision that someone else made in order to do so."

I looked at him, baffled. Was he serious? "Oh yeah, of course, Kyle. What a smart idea. Of course no one would know that the company was breaking the law. Have I hired all morons? How would we not have been caught doing something like that? We would have been better to bury it in the ground. At least then it would have been harder to discover. No, instead we have to throw the shit in the ocean and kill every living thing. They have the damn vessel numbers, Kyle. It's obvious it was us, so how did we not know?" I put my head in my hands, unable to understand what was going on with the people around me.

"Look, Ben, I don't know any more about it than you do right now. But the prosecutor's office will be conducting an investigation into the matter, so we will know soon enough who was behind the whole thing."

"Are you kidding me right now?" I shouted. "I'm being charged, Kyle—do you not understand this? Do you know why? Because they think that I knew the whole time, that it was my own orders."

Kyle sighed. "Yes, I am aware. But I know you had nothing to do with the whole thing, and neither did I. They are going to discover that. You weren't even in the country for god's sake. You will prove yourself in court, and this will all go away. They can't pin something on you when you're an innocent man."

"Right, but how convenient is it that I was out of town when all this was going on? It's as if my alibi was planned."

I got up from the table and went to the window, staring out at the grand view that the boardroom held. Not quite as great as my office view but stunning nonetheless. I needed a drink. I walked to the side table where a decanter stood and poured a brandy for both me and Kyle. I returned to the table and handed Kyle the drink. I sat down beside him and sipped at the brandy, letting the heat burn down my throat, almost cleansing it.

"Kyle, I built this damn company because I believed in something. I had a dream, and this company represented that dream above anything else. Now that dream has been dragged through the mud. Our reputation is smeared and ruined completely. I don't know how we are going to turn it around. Here I am off doing charity work and fundraisers, and someone is throwing poison into the very oceans I am trying to save. It's a bloody joke."

"Ben, it's your obligation to do these works. By doing all the good that you do, you raise the money needed to make a difference. You are not expected to be around here—that's my job, and I'm sorry that something like this happened on my watch. It will be handled—I promise—and I assure you that something like this will never happen again."

"I sure hope not, because I don't think we would survive another public outcry like this one. People want my head on a chopping block."

"It will be over soon, I promise."

"What if it isn't?"

"They can't hang an innocent man, Ben. We just need to do damage control."

I held up my glass and clinked it against Kyle's. We both took another sip. I was lost in my own dark thoughts.

"How would you suggest we clean up this mess? What damage control do you have in mind?"

I could tell that Kyle was deep in thought, and I wondered if that was a good thing or a bad thing. I would do anything I could to save the reputation of this company, but I wondered what he was willing to go through in order to do the same. Kyle was now glancing out the window, and I knew I wasn't going to like what he was about to say. Kyle took another sip of the brandy, and I followed suit. When Kyle turned to me, he only said one word: "Africa."

Confused, I chuckled. "Am I supposed to know what that means?"

"Well, I've already done some research on what kind of damage control we would need at this point to salvage the reputation of not only the company, but yourself as well. We need major PR points to get through this mess. Right now, Africa is in desperate need of people to come in and build schools and hospitals. I've found a great organization that's about to start building in Malawi that could use some help. They need as many workers and supplies as possible. This is where you need to be right now, Ben—helping others and showing the world that you are the same man you were before this mess."

"Going to Africa is going to do that? It's going to fix the problem?"

"Most definitely. No one can argue the importance of all the work you have done over the years, and they won't be able to say it's an act if they see you with hammer and nails out doing it yourself. You're a billionaire—the last place they expect you to be is in Africa. We're going to send a ton of money to the job site, give them all the supplies they need, and then you will fly there and work your ass off. This will really send a message to the world as to what kind of company we are. Not to mention it will show off your strength of character in the midst of a disaster."

I mulled over what Kyle said in my head. It made sense. The last thing I had expected upon my return from vacation was to head off to Africa to work, but it was important that people not forget that I was a humanitarian at heart. I had no idea how that waste got dumped in my name, but I would never be part of such a thing. The amount of money that would have to be spent to salvage the ocean would far outweigh any profit made by the dump. Not to mention the coral and all the sea life destroyed. The thought of it all almost brought me to my knees. Going to Africa was the least that I could do to make amends for what my company did, even if I had been unaware of it all. Besides allowing me to get my hands dirty, it would also do my own soul some good. It had been a while since I had done anything quite like that, and it would help relieve the stress of what was going on. It was probably best I stay away from the company for a short while, otherwise, I might strangle someone.

I looked to Kyle and nodded. "Okay, I'm in. How do we go about doing this?"

"You leave Monday. Leave the rest up to me."

CHAPTER TWO

Ben

Packing for the trip took longer than I expected. I wasn't sure what I needed to bring or how much time I would be away. I did humanitarian efforts all the time, but I had never gone to a site and built a school. I had no idea how long something like that would take. I wasn't sure how much I should pack, and I suddenly wished that I had left the job up to my assistant.

I wondered what Africa was going to be like in general. Hot for sure. The people who would be involved in the building would have no idea about the scandal, and that was a good thing. I hoped to forget about it myself—the last thing I wanted was to be questioned about the whole thing. It was embarrassing enough.

It would be my first time traveling to Africa, and I had to admit I was a little excited about it. Though I had just taken a vacation, this would be something different, something from the soul. It was about time; I usually did fundraisers, but it was well past time that I got my hands dirty. None of my recent fundraisers had had anything to do with Africa, so it would be refreshing to have something new to focus on.

I considered the heat I would have to deal with there and decided only to pack light fabrics and nothing that would cling to me if I started to sweat. I smiled as I added a few more shirts to my suitcase. I was excited to work with my hands. Usually, people just wanted me to throw money at them, and although I was more than happy to do so, this little task would make me feel like a man. A masculine job that entailed putting a structure together—it didn't get much handier than that.

It amazed me that people spent their lives doing projects like that—traveling around, building hospitals for people in need. It was truly selfless. Yet, there were other people who were busy poisoning oceans. I sighed deeply. I really needed to stop thinking about the scandal, or I would surely go crazy. There was nothing I could do about it presently—I had to leave it up to Kyle and the rest of my team to clean things up at the office while I was in Africa. It would be good for me to be out with people, working together as a collective to get a job done. It wasn't just about money for me; I liked to do things that mattered. Although I had planned on getting back to work at the company after my vacation, this was what needed to be done to save the reputation of a company that was my life's work.

The project would be labor intensive, but I wasn't soft. I knew what it meant to work hard for something, and I was up for the challenge, any challenge. It was a good time to get away from the politics of the company, because something had seriously gone wrong. It would be best if I had a clear head when I returned. That way I could be more effective in righting the wrongs that were done. At this point, all I wanted to do was roar all around the office until I got some answers, and that wasn't going to do anyone any good. By going to Africa, I would be able to avoid the media as well, and the only thing they would be able to report about me was all the good I was doing on the trip. It would be really hard for them to say anything bad about me when I was trying to help people out. I could only hope that my community would be able to forgive me for the horrible error my company had made. However, that would not happen until I was able to clear my name.

I STRETCHED out my legs aboard my private jet. There would be some people who would disagree with the fact that I was flying on a private jet to an impoverished country while drinking champagne, but I usually never worried about what people thought—criminal accusations aside, of course. While I was embarking on this trip as a form of damage control and public redemption, I was also giving up a lot of my luxuries to go on this latest adventure, so I was going to enjoy them while I could. Plus, I had worked damn hard to get to where I was in life—I certainly wasn't going to apologize for it now.

Although I was going to an impoverished country, I didn't want to head over there without some of my favorite things. Some of my most favorite luxuries had been sent over so that I could indulge and also give something out to the people I met. There were cigars, chocolate, and my favorite whiskey; I couldn't imagine being gone for long periods of time without these things. I couldn't bear the thought. Some would call me spoiled, but what was the point in being a billionaire if you couldn't make life easier on yourself? I was actually looking forward to sharing my loot with everyone else there. I wasn't sure how long the other workers had been there, but they could probably use some treats at that point—something to keep them going strong.

I hoped to be there only for a few weeks. I would be getting antsy by then to get back to the company and see what was going on and whether I could be of further help there. The last thing I wanted was to be back on the sidelines, having no idea what was happening with my own company. I had made that mistake once before, and I didn't intend to make it again. I just hoped Kyle had a handle on things while I was gone. If anything else went wrong in my absence, heads were going to roll. I could promise that much.

Sitting in my seat, I sipped on the champagne and thought about the life I led and how far I had come in life. I was blessed enough to be able to come and go as I pleased, to pick up at any time and go wherever I wanted on any sort of whim. There were no attachments in my life—no wife or children, nothing to tie me down. I often reflected on these things and wondered if I was really better off without those things. I was about to turn thirty-seven, and I was still living the bachelor's life. Was that a good thing? I couldn't quite be sure.

For a very long time, I had always been happy to just focus on work. Sure, there were women in my life, but none that I fancied enough to stick around forever—they were merely a means of entertainment for me. I often liked to take women on vacation with me as the companionship was enjoyable, but again there was no real desire to see the women again once the vacation was over. It was just for fun, and for a long time that had been okay with me. In fact, rarely had I given much thought to it until recently. Things had been eating away at me for the past few months, and I wasn't sure why. My last vacation was superb, but I always got this inkling that something was missing. But was that a wife and kids? I really didn't know.

I chuckled to myself. Hell, I didn't even have a girlfriend and I was wondering if a wife would complement my life. My life was certainly in a sad state of affairs these days, and I only had myself to blame. I should never have allowed anyone else at the company to have the kind of power to issue a dumping order. I couldn't think about it without feeling sick to my stomach. Now

I was thinking about whether or not I should have a wife. Maybe this was the midlife crisis I kept hearing about. Men went through it more than women did, and I was certainly creeping in on that age. Maybe it wasn't just about having a wife. Maybe I just hadn't met the right woman yet. When she came into my life, maybe things would become clear again for me.

I took women out all the time, often to galas and benefits or a night on the town. I had even on occasion been lucky enough to cook them breakfast in the morning, but I rarely saw the same woman twice. They just didn't interest me that much. It was probably my fault; I had been unattached for so long that I wasn't sure I would know what it was like to spend long periods of time with a woman. Some women would consider me to be a player, but I didn't see it that way at all. I wasn't deliberately out to hurt anyone, and I certainly wasn't opposed to seeing a girl more than once. But she had to spike my interest, keep me intrigued—or at least be passionate about something more important than a new pair of shoes.

The kind of lady I would marry one day, if I ever did marry, would have to be able to keep me on my toes. I needed mental and physical stimulation, and I would offer the same to the woman of my choosing. I wasn't a selfish man. I didn't want a trophy wife; I wanted a woman that could stand on her own while still standing by my side when I needed her. But did such a woman exist? I wasn't sure if she did. I certainly had yet to find her.

Maybe I needed to spend less time on work and more on my personal life. Money was not an issue for me; I had enough to last many generations. My company was my empire, and it offered me a very lavish lifestyle, one that would take care of me for my entire life. I would never need to work a day in my life again if I didn't want to—of course, I would never just hand over the reins of my company, especially not after the shit show that happened that week. If anything, it appeared as if I needed a tighter grip on the reins. My presence at the company was more about having something to keep me busy—plus, I rather enjoyed being in front of the media. There was a time when I was the epitome of philanthropy and public service—that was, of course, before the media got wind that my company had been polluting the ocean.

I rubbed my temples in frustration, unable to even understand how things had gone so wrong. Maybe I should be drinking something stronger than champagne. All I could think about was strangling the idiot that made that monumental decision. If you were going to do something so stupid and thankless, why use vessels with ID numbers attached to them? How stupid could these people be? Of course, it all led back to the company, and now we were in the midst of a national scandal, one that I wasn't sure we would survive. Kyle seemed to think we would be all right, but the damage to the ocean was extensive, and there was no guarantee that we hadn't left some permanent mark.

Whoever was responsible was no doubt shaking in their boots somewhere, hoping that I would never find out. That was impossible, of course; you couldn't pull off something of that magnitude without needing some help and leaving behind a trail. Someone would come forward—if they weren't discovered first. Who knew what was going through this fool's mind? For all I knew, the person might have thought that I would be okay with it. Maybe even applaud him for his genius. There were fake humanitarians all over the world, but I wasn't one of them. I would never be okay with disposing of waste in such a manner.

"Mr. Donovan, would you like more champagne? Your dinner will be out shortly."

I looked up, snapped out of my thoughts. "Yes, of course, thank you. Can I have something a little stiffer though?"

The girl smiled a smile that revealed a lot more than just her happiness to get me another drink. The look she was giving me said she wanted something a little stiffer too. I appraised her, noticing her natural beauty and responding to it. I certainly could use a release and wished I could take her to the back cabin and take her right there. But I had a strict rule against sleeping with staff—it was a terrible idea and always had a way of biting you in the ass, and not in a good way. I didn't need any more scandals in my life, so my staff was always off-limits. The last thing I needed was an angry employee out to seek revenge on me. No, that was something I did not need. The press I was getting now alone was killing me. At the end of the day, it just wasn't worth it to sleep with an employee. It's not like I had trouble finding female companionship, so employees were easy to stay away from.

Plus, I could never be sure if I was being hit on because someone liked me or because they wanted to be Mrs. Billionaire. If you were gonna get married, then why not aim to marry a billionaire? It would be quite a prize for the right girl, and when it came to my staff, I often wondered if they just saw me as a means of moving up in the world. I hated thinking that way, but in my world, it happened all the time. Trophy wives were the thing to have, but no thank you. I had no interest in that at all.

The stewardess returned with my drink looking mildly sulky. She had expected me to take her up on her advances, and when I didn't, she took it personally. That was the dangerous part. She would have been trouble had we slept together and I wronged her. I smiled at her warmly, hoping to ease her wounded ego. The girl was an absolute fox; it was nothing personal, just business. She smiled back at me and hurried off. She wasn't gone long before she returned with my dinner for the evening. The meal looked incredible: grilled salmon and asparagus with small potatoes. I downed the brandy in one gulp, letting it burn my throat on the way down, and then I focused my full attention on the meal before me. The stewardess returned one more time to refill my champagne glass, and then she flitted away.

Most of my favorite meals usually included some form of seafood. I couldn't seem to get enough of it. When it came to maintaining my lean physique, I believed in trying to eat as clean as possible with some treats thrown in here and there. It was just as important to my business and successful lifestyle that I kept my body running smoothly as well—that was how you prevented disease from sneaking in, and when you're building a top company, you can't afford to take sick days. The mind and body always had to be in harmony, and it was my job to take care of that to the best of my ability.

After I devoured the food before me, I suddenly felt exhausted. The goings-on at the company had been of significant mental strain to me, and I was mentally tapped out. I needed a little siesta, and then I would be back in business. I figured it was best to get a nap in while I was still on the jet. Once I arrived in Malawi, I wasn't sure that there would be time for one. I positioned my seat so that it leaned back all the way into a bed.

As I lay back, the stewardess made her way back to me with a pillow and a blanket. It was bizarre watching someone essentially tuck me in for the night, but it was also quite nice. It was the closest I had gotten to true companionship in some time, something that would naturally happen if I'd had a girlfriend. The last thought I had before I closed my eyes was to wonder what it would feel like to have someone in my life that I could take care of and who I knew would also take care of me.

WHEN THE PLANE LANDED, the first thing that hit me when I stepped out was the heat. I knew it would be hot, but I hadn't quite expected this level of heat. I was really in for it, and I was lucky I had done a thorough job of packing.

Malawi was just as beautiful as it was hot. Everywhere I looked it was as if I were on a whole different planet. There was a natural beauty to the place I just didn't see back home—no skyscraper buildings to block the view of what nature had in store for me.

Once we landed, I was ushered through the tiny airport and shuttled to the site at which I would be working. The first thing they did was bring me to the cabin where I would be staying. I wanted to unpack and get settled before things really got crazy for me.

When I arrived at the cabin, I was truly in awe of everything. I couldn't have been happier that I had decided to go on this little adventure and hoped the whole experience would be worthwhile and beneficial for all. The cabin assigned to me had a porch that made me smile immediately. There was something about the thought of working hard all day and then returning to that cabin to an evening whiskey on the porch that filled me with contentment. I could already picture it. It would be marvelous. The cabin was nowhere near luxurious, but it had everything I needed for my stay there.

My first plan of attack was to get unpacked, and then I could take a look around at the site and meet the people in charge. I would get a feel for things that day and then get started with the team the next day. I was pleased to see that all my packages had already arrived. I wanted my belongings and luxury items on hand at all times. I went through the packages and noticed that Kyle had also sent wine, probably just in case I wasn't dining alone. Kyle always thought ahead, and I liked that about him. If I managed to dine alone, I could always give the bottles away. The thing that brought the biggest smile to my face was the bags and bags of individually wrapped candy that I could pass out to any children that I saw. I knew it would make their faces light up as nothing else would.

Once my unpacking was completed, I ventured out onto the porch and took a look around. The heat was therapeutic and made one feel like there was nothing wrong in the world. It wasn't quite the same as lying out on the beach or riding around on my yacht, but the feeling of being in the heat was still very enjoyable. There was a wooden lawn chair on the porch, and I sat down in it. I yawned as I stretched my hands above my head. Yes, there was a lot of good that could be done in a place like this, and I intended on doing what I could while I was there.

The forest surrounding my cabin was lush, a green so bright that it almost hurt to look at the trees. I couldn't believe that such places existed in the world. I just didn't see places like that where I was from. New York really was a concrete jungle compared to this place. I felt blessed to be there and to be in the position where I could help others. I would be able to do a lot of good for the village, and I couldn't wait to get started.

There was a hammock attached to one of the trees, and the sight of it pleased me greatly. I could imagine retiring in it at the end of a grueling day of hammering nails in the heat. I smiled as I thought about the last time I was in a hammock. It must have been when I was a young boy, probably behind my grandparents' place—there was a hammock by the pond. I used to go back there and lay for hours in it, letting the breeze float around me. My own parents had died when I was around ten years old, and I had been raised by an aunt for the most part, often spending time at my grandparents' place. The circumstances of my childhood probably had a lot to do with the fact that I didn't have a lot of attachments to other people.

Well, it was time that I got moving and introduced myself to the people running the site. I doubted I would be working that day, but I wasn't too worried about it either way. If they needed me right away, I would do what I could. Excitement boiled up in me as I thought about making my way to the site and seeing how far along the school and hospital were. I got up from the seat and grabbed a bottle of water before I made my way down the stairs. I followed a path through the lush forest toward what I hoped was the building site. I hadn't seen anyone since I had been dropped off at the cabin, but they had left on the path, so I knew I would find someone eventually.

I was anxious to talk to the head honcho about what the expectations were for me. All the supplies for the site had been paid for by my company and shipped ahead of time, so I wanted to check to make sure they'd gotten everything they needed. It took a lot of supplies to build those two structures, and money meant very little to me—I had plenty to go around and wouldn't miss it.

Thankful for the hat I brought, I could already feel myself building up a sweat as I walked along the path. The sun was beating down even through the trees, and there was not much escape from it. It felt good though; it wasn't overbearing in the least. There was none of the humidity that I was used to during the summer months. The heat was dry, so it never felt as hot as it actually was. In fact it was downright soothing.

The path broke open onto the building site, which was overflowing with people. There was movement and action all around me, and it excited me even more. Everyone was clearly very busy, and a moment was never wasted. The energy in the place was inspiring. There were local villagers around, sitting and watching the volunteers building. It looked as if they were checking out the new people coming and going. The local villagers looked happy, as if they loved the new visitors coming in to change things and hopefully make them better.

I stood on the edge of everything, watching as volunteers unpacked and sorted through the supplies I had sent. I was impressed to see they already had the school's frame well underway. It was already starting to look like something. I felt pride for the camp and what they had accomplished in such a short amount of time, and now I would be part of it. I was going to be able to make a difference, and that was all that mattered to me. As far as I was concerned, the media could kiss my ass. There was no way anyone could believe that I was involved in poisoning the ocean—it truly was ludicrous.

"Mr. Donovan, welcome to the site! We are so happy to have you."

I was startled by a voice beside me and I turned to find a rather pale-looking man. Considering we were in Africa, I was shocked that anyone could remain pale skinned, but sure enough, the man had the pallor of a vampire. His cheeks, however, were flushed, which gave the indication that maybe he just didn't do that well in the heat and hot temperatures. It was a mystery, however, as to why his skin just didn't tan or at least burn. Instead it looked like it lacked almost all color. I put on a warm smile and shook the sweaty palm of the man in front of me.

"Hello, are you the man in charge? I just got here and thought I would take a look around."

"Yes I am, as a matter of fact. The name is Paul, and it is quite a pleasure to meet you. Everyone is so excited that you have decided to join us in our ventures. We couldn't be more grateful for the supplies you sent us. It was very generous of you. As you can see, we are well on our way to having a school, thanks to you."

"The pleasure is all mine, and yes, I did notice that. It looks great and I'm glad to have helped. And please, call me Ben. There is no need to be formal."

"Indeed you are right about that. I am head of the project here, and if there is anything that you require, please come and see me. We have many projects going, all of which are running smoothly. I've been in Africa for over a year now running various projects all over the continent through the very company that you contacted in order to join us here. Were you able to get settled in the cabin?"

"Yes, it's great, thank you. I'm looking forward to getting involved here. I don't think I'll be able to stay as long as you have, but I'll do my best for as long as I'm here," I said with a chuckle.

"Great, that's all good news. Again, we are grateful that you have come to help. There is certainly much to do."

"I wasn't sure if you needed me to start up today or if I would begin in the morning. It's been a taxing day of travel."

"That's totally up to you. Now, what kind of work are you interested in?"

I took a look around. Since my arrival to the site, I felt invigorated and decided to get going right away; there was no need to wait until the morning. Besides, I would only be putting a few hours in before the site shut down for the day and people went off to dinner.

"I'm at your disposal, and I think I'd like to do some work today after all. I'm okay with getting dirty as well—you don't need to give me any special treatment."

Paul laughed. "Good man. That's what I like to hear. How are you with using a hammer?"

"Great. Just show me what you need."

Just then there was a tugging on my leg, and I looked down to see a little girl with chocolate-brown eyes. She was tugging on my pant leg trying to get my attention. She was very skinny, though she didn't appear to be malnourished in any way. I smiled down at her and said, "Hi there, how are you?" The girl smiled back up at me, and I wasn't sure if she understood me at all.

"This is one of our most frequent visitors. Plenty of the children from the nearby villages wander over from time to time. Everyone is very excited that the school is being built, for obvious reasons."

"Do they not have a school?"

"They do and you will see more children filter through during their breaks, but the school is rundown. If there is ever a hard rain, the school floods, and it's not nearly big enough for the number of children in it. They need an upgrade, and this school will mean the ability to learn without worrying about the school falling apart around them. So yes, I believe this little one should be in school, but they get so excited that some venture over whether they are allowed to or not."

I chuckled. "That's fine by me. I'm looking forward to visiting the villages and meeting everyone."

"I'm sure that they would love that. Come with me."

I followed Paul over to a group of people that he introduced me to. It was obvious by the looks they were giving me that they all knew that I was the billionaire funding the project. Not that it bothered me; I would win them over eventually. I just needed to have faith in the situation. I was used to that treatment wherever I went even in the Upper East Side. People treat you differently when you're rich. I was considered one of the elite, and usually everyone wanted a piece of me in more ways than one. But in New York, I was treated with respect automatically. In places like Africa on a job site, I needed to earn the respect first.

It was no big deal though. I was confident that in a few days they would see me as I really was and warm up to me. I was no snob, and they would see that soon enough.

"Now that you've met everyone, Ben, how about we put you to work?"

"Sounds good to me."

The people were smiling around me, but I knew they were

anxious to see if I could actually do hard labor. What they didn't know was that my grandfather used to be a farmer, and I often helped him out on the weekends when I didn't have school. I hadn't always had a privileged life; I had worked hard to get where I am. I followed Paul to where all the tools were being stored. I was handed a hammer and a few boxes of nails.

"You can start over there and work with that group. They'll show you exactly what to do. I'll check on you in a bit, okay?"

"Great, and thanks a lot." I headed to the group, who showed me how they were framing the school. I got to work immediately, hammering nails into the structure, creating a frame as we went along.

There was no doubt about it, the work was truly soul-cleansing, and I knew that going there had been a great idea indeed. The hard work was exactly what I needed to exorcise my demons. I took out all my pent-up aggression on those boards, nailing them in deeper and deeper. I knew I was where I was supposed to be, and when the work was done, I would have a clear head and know exactly what was to be done about my company and the people in it. All the pain and anger from the past week were going into the boards, and I started to feel a weight being lifted off me. By the time Paul came back to retrieve me, we had completely finished the framing of the school, and it looked amazing.

I stood up and joined the people staring at the hard work from the day. I was sweating buckets, but I felt alive for the first time in a long time.

"Great job, everyone. This looks great," I said.

There were lots of high fives and slaps on the back to go around for everyone. They were all pretty proud of the performance that day, and I couldn't blame them. It was amazing what you could do when you had people working together as a team to get a job done. That was a perfect example right there.

As I looked around, I had a great idea. Why not end off my first day there with a bang, something that would make everyone feel wonderful for all the work that was put in that day.

"Excuse me, everyone. It would be my honor if you would all join me at my cabin for dinner tonight. Arrangements have been made for a great spread to be there tonight, and I would love it if you would all join me in having a celebration feast for a job well done. You deserve it, and I hope to see you all there. If the food isn't enough to get you there, I also have alcohol."

There was collective laughter all around, and the sound of it pleased me greatly. They all started to cheer, which made me laugh. "Okay, let's meet at my cabin in an hour. I need to wash off all this sweat."

The crowd started to part, and I made my way back toward the pathway when I was stopped by a kid who couldn't have been more than nineteen. I had been introduced to him before; his name might have been Jeff.

"Hi, Ben. I was just wondering, since you invited us all to dinner and all..."

"Yes?"

"Well, there is another site, the one where they are putting up the hospital. We all usually get together for dinner at the end of the day. Would it be okay if I invited them as well?"

"Of course. We're all in this together after all. I say the more, the merrier."

The kid smiled brightly. "Thanks, man. You are one pretty cool guy."

"Yeah, thanks," I said with a laugh.

CHAPTER THREE

Ben

There were plenty of tables set outside the cabin, and most of them were filled with food from the nearest town. Everything was hot and smelled fantastic. No one was late, probably because you could smell the food for miles and everyone was famished after a hard day's work. I walked around and personally introduced myself to everyone. I wanted them to feel at home with me and not feel like it was a formal affair.

As I was making my rounds, my eyes caught sight of a beautiful woman, her skin lightly tanned. She was easily the most beautiful woman I had ever seen, and her beauty appeared to be natural. She had long, curly red hair tied up in a messy bun that looked sexier than if she had it curled for a gala event. Even from a distance, I could tell she had startling green eyes that seemed to draw in people all around her. She had pouty, sensual lips that looked like they were just begging to be kissed. She looked exotic, though I knew her to be an American as well. She was breathtaking, and it took all my effort to not just stand there and stare at her.

I couldn't tell her age, not that it really mattered to me. All I was able to focus on was how her smile seemed to light up the whole area. Who was that beautiful creature? She must have been from the hospital site because I knew I would have remembered her from my own site. I probably would have followed her around all day. She was with a few friends, chatting amiably and looking around at the feast in amazement.

She was tall and had the build of a professional dancer. I knew I had to try to focus on something else because I was having a hard time taking my eyes off her. She was a stunner, and yet all she wore was cargo pants and a tank top. Even in her plain clothes she could knock the socks off any high-society girl from New York. She was eyeing up the food with her friends, and I was suddenly more pleased than ever that I had arranged the whole thing. The volunteers probably hadn't eaten that well in a while, and I may not have had the chance to meet the girl had I not arranged such a dinner. Whether or not the groups collided in their work, I didn't know, but this event allowed me to make my own introductions to her. I wasn't about to waste any time getting to know her; I didn't want anyone else swooping in before I had the chance to speak with her.

I moved toward her immediately, almost knocking down a few volunteers in the process.

"So sorry," I muttered as I made my way through the crowd.

The closer I got to her, the more beautiful she became—if that were possible. I slowly approached the group she was in as they were gathering up food on their plates. I was close enough to touch her, and I could smell her perfume. It was like sandalwood, and the smell made me want to pull her close to me.

"Hi there. Would you guys care for something to drink?"

She turned to me and smiled, and that was the best gift I

could have been given that day. Her eyes sparkled when she smiled, and it took all my willpower not to pull her in for a kiss. Those lips—I wanted to claim them. I had never reacted in such a way around a woman. I was usually very cool about talking to women, but this one made me think only of my bedroom and what I could do to her there.

"Hi. Ben, is it? We've heard a lot about you. Thank you for inviting us to this party. Everything looks delicious. I'm Katie and I work with the AIDS education initiative. We help people in the villages all around here."

So she wasn't from the other building site. Well, the more, the merrier was what I liked to say. I welcomed all the volunteers to come.

"Katie, that's a pretty name. I'm glad that you could come, all of you."

She blushed and I liked the way her cheeks reddened. It made her even more beautiful.

"I'm famished. I was so thrilled to find out we had a place to go where there was already food ready. I don't even know where to begin."

"Oh, you are very welcome. Food has also been sent to the villages. They should enjoy the festivities as well."

She smiled widely. "Well, that's very sweet of you. I'm sure a hearty meal will do everyone good." She was looking at me with interest, and I wondered if anyone would notice if I snatched her away. I wanted to bring her into the cabin and touch every inch of her.

"Oh, it was nothing. I'm happy to do it."

We stared at each other for a moment, and I wondered if she was feeling the same way that I was. There was a current of electricity charging through my body with her being in such close proximity. It was like we were the only two people there. I didn't even care to talk to anyone else but her. She captivated me, and I wanted to put my mouth on her, badly. She was staring back at me unwaveringly, and I had to wonder if she was having some dirty thoughts herself.

"Well, it was really nice to meet you, Katie."

I held out my hand, and she took it. I shook her hand for an inappropriately long time. We were still staring at each other when I heard her friends giggling. The spell broken, I dropped her hand. Katie was smiling as I tried to compose myself.

"How about that drink?"

She nodded and I proceeded to pour a glass for both her and her friends. I excused myself immediately, not wanting to overstay my welcome. I had no idea what was going through her head, but I knew I needed to clear mine. I went about getting myself a plateful of food and went to find Paul.

Paul was sitting at a table with a few others, and I decided to join them. While I sat there eating, I realized I didn't have much to say. Paul was certainly making up for it as he chatted with everyone, telling all kinds of stories. I was grateful for it because I didn't feel like I could hold my own in a conversation at that point.

The food was fantastic, of course. There were various types of meat, from chicken to ribs to sausages, and a mixture of vegetables and potatoes. There were also various salads and fresh fruit for the taking. It was quite a feast indeed, and everything was fresh. As I ate, however, I had a hard time focusing on anything but my conversation with Katie. We hadn't talked much; it was more about the feeling she gave me when we talked. I kept glancing in her general direction to see what she was doing. She was a bundle of light no matter what she did. She was talking animatedly with her friends, and she seemed like the type of person who really loved life, and that was refreshing to see. I knew I had to have her no matter what. I had never felt such an instant connection to any other woman, and I was determined to make her mine.

As the night wore on, I kept my eye on her and thought of what I could do to win her over. I had caught her eye a few times, and I suspected she had been looking around for me as well. The very thought made me a little hard when I considered that she might want me as badly as I wanted her. All I could think about was undressing her and spreading her legs before me. I needed to find out more about her, see if anyone knew her personally.

I glanced at Paul, who was sipping on some whiskey. "Hey, how well do you know the volunteers that work with AIDS?"

"Oh, very well. I make it a point to know everyone around here. At some point, we end up becoming one big family."

"That's good, especially for those that stay on for long periods of time. What's the story with Katie?"

Paul chuckled. "Are you interested in the girl? You certainly wouldn't be the first man to try to catch her eye. She's gorgeous, which is why there seems to be so much interest in her, of course. Despite that fact, she hasn't shown any interest in anyone else since she's been here. She keeps to herself a lot. I think she's pretty private about her life."

I nodded, taking it all in. "She's not actually a girl, is she?"

Paul couldn't help but laugh out loud, drawing attention to our table. Katie glanced my way, and our eyes locked. I held her gaze for a beat, feeling aroused all over again. What was with this woman and the power she had over me?

"No, of course not. Though we do get some volunteers who are young, I think she's around twenty-eight and quite a bright girl. As far as I know, she's taking a break from her life to find herself a bit before going back to the real world. But I guess that's what we're all doing here, isn't it, Ben?"

I met his gaze and knew that he had heard all about the

scandal going on back home at my company. I wondered who told him and whether others at the site knew about it as well. I supposed it was bound to happen no matter what, but I had hoped for a little time off from discussing it. I could only hope that Paul, and whoever else knew, didn't think badly of me. I would at least like the benefit of the doubt in the situation. I had, after all, done nothing wrong. The last thing I wanted was for anyone to believe the rumors about me. It was a horrible situation, and I didn't like the idea that I could come to a place like Africa for a break only to have it all follow me there.

I nodded slowly. "Yeah, you're right. That's usually why people find themselves in a place like this. Working off their sins, I suppose, or trying to save the world, yet sometimes I think the two are often connected."

"True enough, Ben. I can tell you are a good man though."

"I appreciate that, Paul. As are you."

Paul smiled and picked up his plate as he left the table. People started filtering out for the evening, the sun long gone now, leaving behind the moon for company. It was time for everyone to retire for the night as work started again at 6 a.m. I knew what I had to do; I wasn't the kind of man that believed in having regrets. I stood up from my table and threw my plate in the garbage. I then made my way over to the table that Katie was in the middle of leaving.

"Katie, I wondered if you would like to stick around and have another drink with me?"

She smiled warmly, and her friends giggled beside her. They left immediately, knowing full well what Katie was going to say. It made me wonder if I had been the topic of conversation at their table for the evening.

"That would be wonderful, thank you. You can't keep me out late though—I'm not a morning person and I need my beauty sleep." She laughed as she said it, and I had never heard anything more pleasing.

"I doubt that." I motioned for her to head up to the porch, and she did so, finding herself a seat against the railing. I went ahead and poured us both a glass of wine and handed her one. She took a sip and looked out at the night. The sounds all around us were nothing like what you would hear in the city; it was actually kind of magical. I sat down beside her, ignoring the chair. I didn't want to be that far away from her.

"Tell me, Katie, what brought you to Africa? Tell me more about the AIDS volunteer work you are doing."

"Well, for the most part it's education based. We spend most of our time at the current school teaching the kids. AIDS is a real problem here, and we hope to try to stop it from affecting future generations. We are trying to teach the kids about sex and how the disease is spreading out of control. We hope to prevent it from happening. At this point, all we can do is educate them and tell them how to avoid it."

"I'm surprised that such a young girl is so invested in a project like this."

"I'm not that young," she said with a laugh. She stared at me long enough to drive her point home. Every part of my body took the hint.

"I just meant that someone as young as you should be out enjoying her youth, going out and having fun with friends and going to parties."

"Well, I did do all that, but that stuff gets old. I want my life to have a purpose. I don't want to be club-hopping all through my twenties."

I nodded, watching her carefully. Paul was right; she had a good head on her shoulders.

"So why come here?"

She turned to me. "No, you first. We all know you to be quite a wealthy man, Ben. What brings you to Africa to slum with the rest of us?"

I chuckled. "It's hardly slumming it. Something unexpected happened at my company recently that really had me reevaluating a lot of things. Trouble is brewing, I'm afraid, and I needed a break from it all. This is my temporary escape, somewhere that I can do some good while allowing myself to get a clear perspective on things. Plus, it was time that I got my hands dirty for a change instead of constantly writing checks. It's nice to come and meet a situation head on instead of just throwing money at it. By being here, I can truly see what's going on and where I can help the most."

"Yeah, I can understand that. Well, to some degree—I don't think I have any idea what it's like to be in charge of a billion-dollar company. Your lifestyle is very different from mine, I'm sure."

"Maybe." I smiled. "Now it's your turn."

She looked into her hands, suddenly looking very sad. "I came here because I realized I had an amazing life, and I felt guilty for it. Sounds crazy, I know. All my friends back home thought I was nuts, but I've just been so blessed in life that I wanted to make my life matter more, I guess."

"Interesting. Explain it to me."

She smiled and took a deep breath, looking quite wistful about what she was going to say. "Oh, there's no terrible past haunting me or anything. People just look at my life and think I should have this whole journey attached to it, and I don't."

"What sort of story do they expect you to have?"

She laughed. "I guess I'm not really explaining myself very well, am I?"

I smiled.

"Well, my family is completely normal and all well educated. A lot of people here are running away from something. I'm not.

My life is normal and happy. I'm educated as well. I went to university for fashion, and that's what I plan on focusing on when I get back. I already have clients lined up waiting for my designs. Some weren't too happy that I decided to take a hiatus."

"You sound like you have a promising future, so I'm not sure what you feel guilty about."

She giggled. "I didn't expect you to be so easy to talk to." I smiled at her, glad that she found comfort in talking to me. I had to admit that I enjoyed talking with her as well.

"Hold your thought while I pour us some more wine." I left her sitting on the porch while I went to fetch another bottle of wine. I didn't fill the glasses too much this time, as I didn't want her to be hungover in the morning and it was getting late. I returned to the porch and handed her the glass.

"I hope you don't feel guilty about being successful, Katie, because that's something that you are supposed to take pride in."

"I knew a girl once who had to struggle for everything she had. When we were in school together, she wrote a paper on the African American culture. It was rather beautiful." She paused and I waited for her to finish. I was completely intrigued by her; I could listen to her talk like that all night, even though I couldn't help but think how much fun other things could be as well.

"I guess knowing this girl is where the guilt comes in for me. She ended up going into politics while I studied fashion. We got together once, and she ended up showing me a video of the things that were going on in Africa. She is a big advocate, and she wanted me to be more involved in the world than just fashion. It made me realize how much I had in life while there were others who had nothing at all. Do you know what I mean? I just knew that I needed to give something back, to try to make a difference even if it was just in some small way. So I left my sister in charge of the ordering of my designs, and I imagine by the time I get back I'll have a whole fashion company in the works. Which of course is very exciting."

"You have a lot to be proud of, I hope you realize that. Your parents must be very happy with you."

"Actually, no, they're not at all right now. They worked really hard in their life to give me a better life, something grander than the one that they had. They wanted me to enjoy the life they gave me, not come here and feel guilty about it," she said with a laugh.

"I guess I can understand that. Parents always want what's best for their kids, and they just want you to be successful. This is temporary, of course, and they will see you happy in your business and the rest won't matter."

"Thank you for saying that."

I chuckled, not wanting the talk to get too serious. I was surprised by how the conversation had turned. I wasn't exactly the type of person that liked to dig deep when I first met someone—of course, things just felt different with Katie.

"Well, you can't be much older than I am," she uttered.

"A little bit. I'm thirty-six. Plus, I have a lot of experience, probably more so than you."

"Experience in what?" she whispered. It wasn't so much that she whispered but how she whispered that caught me off guard. It was like she had lost her breath—it was kind of hot. I didn't know what to say to her; she had rendered me speechless. I felt like I was losing control of my thoughts and wasn't sure that it was the right time to make a move on her.

"I really feel like you understand me, Ben, and that's a rare thing to find. You make me want to tell you things that I shouldn't."

She was looking up into my eyes. "Oh, I definitely like you too, probably more than I should."

"Well, we don't always have to be good, do we? We can just follow how we feel, can't we?"

I stared into those insanely green eyes as they bore into mine. I could feel myself growing hard, and my eyes found her lips. All I wanted to do was take her right then and there, put my hot mouth on her body. We had just met, and I worried we would be starting something we couldn't finish. I didn't want to hurt her. I wasn't exactly used to having attachments. And though we wouldn't be working together exactly, we would be working close by, and I didn't want to cause a mess with the important work we were both doing. The last thing I needed were rumors going around about the two of us. The problem, however, was that all I could do was think about how good it would feel to slide inside of her. I didn't think I would be able to get that thought out of my head.

"I should tell you, Ben, that no man has been able to give me an orgasm before."

Before I could process what she just said to me, she got up and made the decision for me. She latched her mouth on to mine, and the fire that lit between us was intense. Katie gasped inside my mouth, and my loins burned for her. My hands went into her hair, pulling her closer to me. I kissed her deeply, finding her tongue and sucking on it gently. She moaned and the sounds she made had me rock hard in a second. Oh yes, I would have her tonight. I needed to hear her moan all night long.

I stood up then and pulled her body to mine. I kissed down to her chin and trailed kisses along her neck, sucking on her. Her hands found the bulge in my shorts, rubbing me hard, causing a friction that drove me insane. The knowledge that she was eager for my cock drove me half-mad. I picked her up, carrying her into the cabin, and laid her out on my bed.

I pulled off her tank top and unclasped her bra. Her breasts dropped deliciously from the bra, and I bent down to suck on her nipples. She gave a guttural moan and I sucked even harder. I planned on giving her an orgasm she would never forget. I couldn't believe that she had never had one before. Who were these men she was sleeping with? She was so responsive; the other guys she'd been with must've been totally clueless.

She pushed me away to tear off her shorts, and I glimpsed a pair of white lace panties before she slid them to the floor. I couldn't believe how badly I wanted to fuck her right then. She drove me insane.

I dropped to the floor in front of her, spreading her legs as she leaned back on the bed. Her pussy was so pink it made me crazy. She was already wet, and I slid a finger inside her, feeling her drip down my finger. I bent forward, placing my lips on her clit. She gasped in surprise as my lips touched her pussy. I loved the taste of her, and I drank in her juices as I felt them against my mouth.

I licked her like she was the tastiest ice cream and plunged my tongue inside her. I ached to fuck her, but having this taste of her was hard to pass up. I licked her pussy all over; having her cum in my mouth would be the ultimate victory. I moaned deeply. Licking her pussy made me so horny.

"Katie, you are so hot. I love this."

She writhed against me, and I knew I had to have her soon.

"Oh my god, Ben." She moaned my name, and it was just about the best sound I had ever heard. I leaned in and sucked her clit, forcing her to thrash beneath me. "Right there, baby, that feels so good." Katie made a high-pitched sound I had never heard before, and knowing I brought her so much pleasure had me bound and determined to give her the elusive orgasm she'd never had with a man.

"I'm so close... oh god..." Katie grabbed the back of my head and pushed up harder against my mouth. I sucked her good while fucking her with my finger.

With an earth-shattering scream, Katie came all over my finger and mouth. I pulled out and looked into her dazed eyes. Her face was flushed from her orgasm, and I felt a swelling sense of pride and satisfaction. Knowing I was the only man to ever bring her to that state made me harder than I'd ever been in my life. I wanted my cock in her pussy the next time she came.

Katie panted heavily, trying to catch her breath, but she couldn't have made it clearer that she wanted the same thing as I did with the next words that came out of her mouth. "Please, Ben, I want you inside me."

I never wanted a lady to beg. I would give her exactly what she wanted. I pulled Katie up and turned her over. She gasped in excitement as she bent over for me, her tight round bottom in my face. I bent down and kissed her bottom, moving in real close to her. I was rock hard and couldn't wait to plunge inside her pink little pussy.

I drove deep inside her, making her moan loudly. She was tight and wet, and I really had to control myself or I would lose myself completely inside her.

"Ben, I need it."

Her ass looked glorious before me as I plunged deeper inside and moved within her. She called out to me loudly, and I briefly wondered if there was anyone within earshot. I couldn't have cared less, however—let the whole village hear us. I was fucking an amazing woman, and I wouldn't stop for anything.

Katie was so sensitive from her first orgasm that she came against my cock with a couple of thrusts. I continued to rock inside her until I spilled into her as well. I leaned down on top of her back, breathing heavily into her hair.

"Oh, Katie that was incredible."

"You bet your ass it was." She giggled underneath me. I

rolled off her and lay down on the bed. She lay beside me, and we were both silent, thinking about what had just happened between us. She rolled onto my chest and nuzzled into it. I wrapped my hands around her and kissed her on the top of her head.

"Yes, that definitely was amazing." We fell asleep tangled up in each other's arms.

CHAPTER FOUR

Ben

The next morning, I awoke well before dawn and felt a beautiful woman in my arms. I pulled her in tighter and felt myself grow hard again. I wasn't sure what was going to happen between us after the night we'd had together, but I didn't want to pass up morning sex with her. It was the best way to start the day after all, and there weren't too many women that could make me hard instantly. I wanted to fuck her before we went off to work. I nuzzled into her neck until I felt her stir. She moaned as I pressed my hard cock against her bottom.

"I need you badly, Katie. My god, it hasn't even been twenty-four hours and I need to be inside you right now. I would love to give you more orgasms—I know you've been denied them for far too long."

Her breath caught and she couldn't even respond to me. What a turn-on to have a woman react to me in that way, to show me that she needed me that much. My body was warm all over at the thought of taking her again.

She turned over to me and kissed me, her tongue sliding gently into my mouth and touching my tongue. Electricity hit me and I started to feel hot. Oh god, what was with this girl? She was just so incredible that I couldn't keep my hands off her, and I was sure she felt exactly the same way.

She smiled up at me again, her eyes watching me intensely. "I would like you to touch me."

I groaned. "Baby, that's all I want to do. I want to have that sweet ass in my hands once again. You are so hot, Katie."

She moaned. "Oh Ben, that is so sexy. I love the way you talk to me."

She moved closer to me and rubbed the front of my underwear, pressing her hand against my cock. Talk about easy access. She was kneading hard against me until I felt myself growing harder still. I had already been plenty hard when I woke up, and feeling myself grow turned me on that much more. She could make me rock hard so easily. I groaned at her touch, and my hands slowly went down her body and grasped her ass.

I smiled. "I can't help myself. I just can't get enough of you."

"I know how you feel." She giggled.

She raised herself in the doggy position. She knew exactly what she wanted.

"You want me to fuck you from behind? I'm going to make you feel incredible."

Her firm ass was there for me to take, and I wanted to slip in from behind nice and deep. She was completely perfect. I couldn't take it; I wanted to pound her hard from behind and make her say my name again and again.

I was going to fuck her really good. I squeezed her breasts from underneath, and she released a soft cry. My head was filled with this girl, and I knew I wouldn't have been able to go to the site that day and try to work without dipping my cock into her first.

My fingers found her opening. I loved how she was always ready for me, her pussy wet with need for me. "Oh baby, you are already so wet."

I plunged a finger inside her and fucked her gently while she mewled in my arms. I was already addicted to her, and I needed to fuck her more than anything. I knew she felt exactly the same way; I could practically feel her need for me. She made me lose all sense of reasoning—it was like there was a fog that surrounded us when she was around and she was all that mattered. She wanted me and she was going to get all of me. I lifted her up and flipped her over.

"Don't worry, sweetheart, I'm going to fuck you good doggy-style—I just want something first."

She lay back onto the bed and spread her legs. Seeing her wet pussy right there before me almost drove me half-mad. She looked good enough to eat, and I planned on licking every inch of her soaking pussy. I bent down and started to slowly lick her opening, sticking my tongue inside of her.

"Baby, you are so hot."

She writhed against me, and I knew I had to have her, to fuck her really good. I sat up and pulled her up to me. She turned around and leaned forward, her firm ass high in the air as I slid inside her warm pussy and felt the deepness. I groaned with pleasure. She felt amazing and I doubted that I would ever tire of having my cock inside of her. I was so deep—I couldn't believe how incredible she felt.

"Harder, Ben, please."

That was all it took. I pumped against her hard, feeling every inch of her. Her fingers clenched against the bed sheets as waves of pleasure went through her. She called out my name over and over again, and it was music to my ears. She wanted it hard, and I would bet she would be sore later—I would guarantee that much. I fucked her hard, listening to her whimper my name. I pumped harder while I reached over and rubbed her clit. She was so wet that my fingers slid over her pussy easily. I bent forward and kissed her shoulder, nipping it gently. I fondled her breasts from underneath, loving the feel of her soft skin.

I could feel her tightening around me, and I knew she was going to cum again. I pumped faster and she muffled her cries of pleasure into the pillows. Oh, she was good, really good. Her orgasm broke through, and she whimpered as she finished. I continued to thrust into her; I wasn't ready to give up yet.

I rubbed her ass while I was still inside her. "You truly are a gift to me, Katie. I can't get enough of you."

I pulled out of her and she quickly flipped over, surprising me. She pushed me back down on the bed and straddled me. It was the hottest sight I had seen in some time. I couldn't believe it was possible, but I was growing even harder watching her. She bent down and took my cock into her mouth. I moaned as she sucked hard.

"Whoa! Baby, easy, or you are going to make me cum." I almost lost control. She sucked me hard, and I whispered, "What an amazing blow job, baby." Her tongue swirled around my cock as she took me in deeper into her mouth, my cock hitting the back of her throat. I groaned as she made my cock start to throb. She continued sucking until I begged her to stop.

"C'mon, baby, I want to fuck you again." She rose from her position and kissed me on the mouth. Her mouth on me was hot and wet. I slid my hand to her pussy and rubbed at her clit.

"Oh, sweetheart, you are so wet."

"Oh Ben, you do that to me. I can't stop thinking about you inside me. I just have to have you again. And it's my turn to make you feel good."

I smiled, loving the way she talked to me. When she talked dirty, it drove me wild. We were kindred spirits.

"I can't wait to fuck you again, Katie. I was so disappointed to have to leave your pussy." I went to lift her up onto my cock when she stopped me. I sat back but she pushed me right back down. I laughed, enjoying the look on her face. She had the power now, and she was enjoying every bit of it. I looked her up from top to bottom, finally resting my eyes on her perfectly shaved pussy. My cock was hard and ready, and she knew I didn't want to wait any longer. She climbed on top of me and kissed me passionately, and my hands found her breasts.

She was blowing my mind. "You want to cum inside me so badly, don't you, baby?"

"God, yes, Katie! I want to feel inside your pussy so badly."

Her kisses went from my mouth to my jaw line, nipping the side. She trailed kisses down my chest and licked the trail that led to my throbbing cock. She slid down the bed, wanting my cock once again. I was just going to have to wait a bit longer it seemed. The torture would be worth it.

She licked and sucked the tip of my cock teasingly. "You little devil you."

She was gorgeous as she lapped at my cock while looking me straight in the eyes. I was slowly losing my mind. She quickly climbed on my lap once again and moved above me, plunging my cock inside of her. She gasped above me, and I groaned in pleasure. I watched as she rode me slowly, moving on my cock in a torturously slow rhythm. Her red hair fell over her breasts as she bounced on my cock and I had the best view in the house. I put my hands on her hips and ground her onto me. Katie moaned like a kitten, and the sound drove me crazy. She tightened around my cock, and I knew she was about to spill around me. She came quite vocally, and I laughed, loving the sound of it.

"I love the sound of you cumming, Katie." She smiled down at me and rode me harder. She took my hand and sucked on my middle finger while she rode me hard. "Wow, baby, that is so hot."

She began to ride my cock harder, her body grinding into mine. The tension inside was building, and I was going to blow with her while she was in complete control over my orgasm. "Oh god, Katie, that feels so good." I came inside her hard, and she continued to rock on me, riding me to one of the most intense orgasms I'd ever had.

I was spent, and she felt wondrous on top of me. She bent forward and licked my mouth before kissing me hard. She climbed off and opened up a drawer to grab some Kleenex to clean off. Being with Katie had been amazing both times. It felt glorious being inside of her; despite the incredible orgasm I'd just had, I was a little sorry that it was over. I could smell her perfume around us as she climbed on my lap again and held me close to her.

"You smell fantastic, Katie."

"Thank you." She looked down into my eyes with a coy smile.

As I stared into her beautiful eyes, I couldn't help but wonder again how she'd been able to make it to the age of twenty-eight without ever having a man bring her to orgasm. "Can I ask you something personal?" I hoped she would indulge me and not think I was being rude—I had this urge to know more about her, and I was used to getting what I want.

She chuckled. "I'd say we're on more than personal terms at this point—and let me guess, you want to know about the orgasm thing?" I nodded and she continued. "You know, it's not for a lack of trying. I've had my share of partners, and most of our encounters were enjoyable, but I guess there was just something missing. A lack of intensity, I guess." She shrugged, and her smile widened. "Until now, that is."

I smiled back, feeling pretty flattered that she had enjoyed herself so much with me. Just thinking about it all made me want to go at it again, but I knew we had other things we should be doing instead. "Maybe we should consider getting to work."

"Maybe... That is a valid point, but I think I want to fuck you again." She gave me another huge smile, and I was lost.

CHAPTER FIVE

Ben

When I finally managed to get out of bed that day, I'd never felt better. In fact, I felt downright incredible. The night before I had slept like the dead with the most beautiful creature in my arms, and then the morning arrived and we had barely wanted to get out of bed at all. Despite the hard work of the day before, I had woken up feeling more refreshed than I had in a long time.

After we had slept together again that morning, Katie had slipped out of bed, dressed quickly, and left without a word. She was truly a mysterious creature, but I adored every part of her. It was crazy to think we'd known each other less than a day. I already felt such a connection to her. The sex had been mind-blowing, to say the least, and all I wanted to do was find her and drag her back to bed.

I was ready to start my day, and I was grateful that the day hadn't been completely wasted. Despite the fact that we had continued romping after we woke that morning, it was only 8 a.m. when I started getting ready to go out to the site. I hoped that her quick departure didn't mean that she was upset about anything. She was an incredible woman, and the last thing I wanted was for her to have any regrets about the time we had spent together.

I washed up in the basin that had been left out for me. I dressed quickly in a light linen shirt and some shorts. I wanted to speak with Katie again before I went back to work, just to make sure that we were on the same page about everything. I wasn't willing to just move on after such an explosive night together and needed to make sure Katie was feeling the same. I didn't want any misunderstandings or hurt feelings getting in the way of what could be an incredible couple of weeks.

I knew I would have to venture over to the old school in order to find her, but I was confident I could find it easily. From what I'd heard, it wasn't too far off from the new site, especially since the schoolchildren often found their way over for a visit. I followed another path that led me to the current school, and when I laid eyes on it, my mouth dropped open. It was in worse shape than I had imagined it to be. With the foundation crumbling and the roof falling in, I was appalled to think that the children spent any amount of time in there trying to learn. If a building such as that were in New York, it would be condemned, and yet that was the only building they had currently to use as a school.

Shaking my head in dismay, I approached a group of people that I recognized from the dinner last night. I asked them if they knew where Katie was, and they mentioned that they hadn't seen her at the site. I took a quick look around and realized she wasn't at the site at all. When I approached her giggling friends, they claimed they had no idea where she was, although judging by the looks on their faces, they weren't exactly being truthful with me.

When I checked my watch, I realized that I was making myself even later to the work site, and I didn't want to appear as if I was lazy and didn't want to work. I would have to try to find Katie after the workday was complete, or hope that I would see her at dinner when everyone collected together.

The sun was beating down on me, and I was grateful that I had thought to bring a hat with me. Otherwise, I would have been in real trouble. Everyone was sweating buckets from the heat, and although we accomplished a lot of work by lunch, I was downright exhausted from the heat. I found that the heat itself was more physically taxing than actually wielding a hammer. All I could think about was stepping into a cold shower and washing away the grime of the day, but I knew that would not be happening anytime soon.

When the lunch bell rang, everyone else headed to the lunch table while I decided to take another stab at finding Katie at the old school. She had been all I could think about for the whole day, and I thought it was odd that I had not seen her yet. Where would she have gone if she didn't go to her own job site that morning?

I grabbed two bottles of water from the job site and drank both of them by the time I made it to the old school. I hoped that Katie would be there because I knew I wouldn't be able to stop thinking about her until I found her and spoke with her. Never before had my thoughts been so consumed with one woman. Usually, I slept with a girl and then never thought about her again, but that wasn't the case with Katie. I felt the urge to be around her all the time, or to at least know she was okay after the night and morning we had spent together.

The fact she had left without so much as a kiss goodbye that morning had bothered me. I had to admit that I was a little more intrigued with Katie than I was with most other girls. There was just something about her; I couldn't quite put my finger on it. There was no doubt she was hot and quite a little sex kitten in the bedroom, but there was more to her than that. She had ambition and she was smart as hell, and I liked everything about her.

When I arrived at her site, I saw her immediately and relief flooded me. She was playing outside with the children, and they were all laughing and chasing each other around.

I didn't waste any time and walked right up to her. She smiled as she saw me approaching, though I must have looked a sight. Being out in the heat and sweating, I hoped that I at least didn't stink badly.

"Ben, I didn't expect to see you. Welcome to the school—have you seen it yet?"

"Yes, I was here this morning. It's quite a sight. I'm happier than ever that they decided to build a new one. That one looks rather fearsome—I feel bad for the children inside it. Are they safe?"

"Yes, for the most part. We've had the engineers look it over, and they said that nothing will fall down on them anytime soon. But obviously, the sooner we get them out of there, the better. The teachers will often come outside for lessons, unless it rains, of course."

"I see. Do you think we could talk for a moment... alone?"

She smiled warmly and looked at the children that were swarming us. "Go back inside, children—the lesson will be starting shortly. Julie will start things off, and I will be in soon enough."

"Take some of these with you, kids." I handed them a handful of chocolates, and they squealed in delight. They ran off toward the school, ripping open chocolate as they scattered. I had never seen happier kids.

Katie laughed as she watched them run into the school. "Well, that's one way to get them moving." She looked up at me. "You look like you've been working hard today."

"Yeah, no kidding." I laughed. "I can't believe the heat today. I think I've sweated off ten pounds today."

"Yes, the heat takes some getting used to."

"I just wanted to chat with you a bit, Katie. You left so abruptly this morning that I just wanted to make sure that everything was okay with you."

"Oh, did it bother you that I left?"

"No, of course not." I chuckled. "I guess I just wanted to make sure you didn't have any regrets about what we did."

"Why would I have any regrets? You made me feel quite good. The first man to give me an orgasm. That's no easy task."

I broke out into a grin, impressed with the things that came out of her mouth. It was the last response I had expected, and she didn't appear the least bit uncomfortable or awkward around me. She had a twinkle in her eye that made me want to drag her into the forest and take her right then and there. She was an absolute fox when she smiled.

"Well, that's a relief."

"There's no need to be concerned at all, Ben. I didn't want to overstay my welcome. Plus, we both needed to get to work. I was quite late by the time I made it to my site." She paused for a moment. "Besides, I'm not really sure what's going on between us."

"You could never overstay your welcome. Just so you know."

"Well, I appreciate that." She giggled.

"In fact, I would love it if you allowed me to touch your body anytime that I wanted to."

She gasped, but then a smile formed on her face. She didn't respond to me, but she also didn't say no.

CHAPTER SIX

Ben

A week passed and every day just got better. Every moment that Katie and I weren't spending at the job sites we were spending together, and it was the most fun that I'd had in some time. She was playful and we spent a great deal of time laughing and talking through the night. However, that wasn't the only thing we did—in fact, I filled her with my cock every night, and sometimes we would sneak off together at lunch and roll around in my sheets.

Katie was like a drug to me, and I just couldn't get enough of her. We never got bored of each other, and every time we joined, it felt like it was the first time. I never got sick of taking off her clothes. She loved to give me random acts of oral that just sent me to the moon and back. She would often do things to my cock that made me see heaven. She was an incredible lover, and it only added to her mysterious appeal. When we got together, we would immediately head to the bedroom, where we would fuck in every conceivable position. My lust for her was insatiable. We could rarely have a peaceful dinner together—it was only after I had satisfied my hunger for her that we could then sit and enjoy a meal, and sometimes we skipped eating altogether.

I turned as she walked into my cabin during one particular lunch break. It sometimes felt like I barely even ate lunch because I would much rather spend my break worshipping Katie's body. She came to me immediately, and I looked down into her beautiful green eyes. I drank her in—I never wanted to forget her face. It haunted my dreams at night.

I brushed the hair out of her face and stepped just an inch closer, invading her personal space. My heart was beating madly, and I couldn't believe how horny she made me still, even after we had slept together so many times that I'd lost count. I never grew bored with Katie the way I had with other women I had slept with, and that told me a lot about the chemistry we shared. She was like a shot of heroin I needed to have right then.

I wondered how often people got to be with someone who made them feel this good, this incredible. Katie made me feel like I was alive even when we weren't together, and I knew a lot of my friends didn't have that feeling with their significant others. Did that mean that they settled for something less? The thought horrified me, and I knew that was why I had stayed single for so long. I didn't want to give up my bachelor lifestyle for anything less than the best.

"Would it shock you if I told you that I wanted you the moment I first laid eyes on you at the dinner, hanging out with your friends?" I whispered in her ear. "I thought you were the prettiest thing that ever walked into my life."

"No, it was pretty obvious you had a thing for me." She laughed. "I mean, I did end up in your bed that very night. But I feel the same way, just so you know."

Her words excited me, and I knew right then I was going to kiss those pouty lips—I was going to make them swollen from my mouth. I needed to taste her—it's all I thought about as I worked away tirelessly at the school. We had been making huge progress the past few days, and things were really starting to shape up.

She locked eyes with me, and I knew she felt the same burning desire for me as I felt for her. I kissed her then and tasted a hint of strawberry. The combination of her taste and the feel of her soft lips excited me, and I felt an urgency to be inside her. My hands found her breasts, and I squeezed them hard enough to let her know what was coming. She moaned a guttural noise that told me that she needed me too. My arms encircled her and fumbled while I pulled off her tank top.

"Ben, maybe we shouldn't. We've been sneaking away for weeks—we should go back. Someone will come looking for us one of these days."

"I don't care—and do you really think people don't know about us? Of course they do. I want you so badly, and if I don't have you, I might lose my mind."

She looked so nervous that I kissed her mouth gently, coaxing her back to me. She moaned again as I started to undress her. I couldn't wait to have her naked body in front of me.

I cared for her, there was no doubt. I kissed her mouth again, my erection growing. She rubbed her hand against my hard cock the way she knew I loved, and it felt like it was going to burst out of my pants.

"You are going to feel so good in a minute, I promise you, Katie. I'm going to fuck you really good, baby."

I wanted to feel her pussy more than ever now. The fact that she wanted to give herself to me regularly made my cock throb. I picked her up in my arms and carried her over to my bed—it was practically our bed at that point. She rarely slept in her own cabin anymore, opting to sleep with me at night.

I pushed her down on the bed and spread her legs. Her

pussy looked so delicious—I ate her out often just for the fact that I loved the way she tasted. I slipped my hand between her legs. She was already wet and eager for me. I loved that about her. She got excited so easily, and feeling her moist pussy drove me wild. I rubbed her clit gently, moving my thumb in a circular pattern, caressing her gently at first and then harder. She moaned softly, and it turned me on so much. I looked up at her from between her legs, and she was watching me intensely. She was such a hot fuck.

"Oh, Ben."

"I'm going to make you feel really good, Katie." She loved it when I said that to her.

All she could do was moan when I slid a finger into her already wet pussy. I fingerfucked her and felt her pussy getting wetter around my finger. She always got really wet, and it made me insanely horny. I couldn't take it anymore when I heard her whisper, "Please, I want more." I planned on giving her much more.

I slid my finger out and started undoing my shorts. I dropped them to my ankles but didn't bother to get out of them. She lay back on the bed and spread herself before me. Her mouth was swollen from my kisses, and she waited for me. I bent forward so I could suck on her nipples. I took one in my mouth and sucked on it while her back arched. I couldn't get enough of her little hot body, and if a day ever went by where we didn't sleep together, I was sure that I would go completely mad.

When I slid inside her, I made sure to be gentle, but she was so tight I worried I might hurt her anyway.

She whispered, "I love how big you are."

Fuck that was so hot. I almost pushed all the way in after that but focused on not filling her too roughly. I gently rocked into her until I filled her pussy completely. She moaned in delight, and I rode her slowly at first, kissing her face and talking to her softly. When I knew she was okay, I pumped her a little faster until she was crying out my name. It sounded just the way I remembered it—it was my favorite part of fucking her. She was so incredibly hot that just the act of fucking her made me horny to fuck her again. I fucked her a little harder, my hips jerking wildly as I started losing all sense of reason being inside her warm pussy while she screamed my name. She exploded around my cock as I rode her hard, and I spilled into her soon after.

I lay on top of her for a moment, breathing in her sweet perfume. I lifted my head and kissed her deeply. I gently kissed her face, her throat, and her neck, trailing kisses all the way to her chest.

"How are you doing, Katie?"

She smiled. "That was very good. I think we get better every single time. I really can't get enough of you inside me."

"I agree, it feels incredible. Your pussy feels so good. "

I sat up and exited her gently before cleaning myself off. I looked at the time. "Well, we are definitely late—our lunch break was over some time ago." I laughed like a man who had little care in the world—and at that moment I didn't.

Katie had felt incredible, and I wouldn't have missed fucking her for anything. I was tempted to go at her a second time just to feel inside her again. When I was inside her and she was squeezing me tight, I felt a sense of completeness that nothing else could give me.

But I had obligations now, and I needed to be at the site to finish the day. It was important to the whole team that I not flake on them, even though I was sure that everyone knew about us and found it rather amusing. The fact that when one of us disappeared, the other followed shortly after was a pretty good indication that we were always together. Plus, we always got looks when we were at the site together—not that I cared. The looks weren't malicious. If anything, I felt that people were just happy for us and found the situation funny, especially when we would disappear together.

Katie sat up and started getting dressed and fixing her hair. She totally looked as if she had just had sex—there wasn't much she could do to fix her hair. She was so hot that I continued contemplating giving it to her a second time, but I knew we didn't have time for that. Someone would eventually come looking if we decided not to show up at all. Plus, it would be very disrespectful to do so. The last thing I wanted was to get a reputation for being a playboy when I was supposed to be building a school. I was proud of my accomplishments with the school thus far and didn't want to disappoint anyone.

I helped Katie finish getting dressed, and I gave her a little tap on the backside. She grinned as she finished getting ready. I started to get dressed myself, wishing that we had more time. I watched her try to straighten things out as I pulled on my shirt and shorts. She reapplied her strawberry lip balm, and I hoped her lips wouldn't look so red by the time we got back to the job site. She definitely looked like she had been kissed an awful lot, and just thinking about those kisses made me semi-hard again. No matter how hard she tried to straighten herself out, she still looked like she had just been fucked. I liked that look—I would be fine if she always looked that way. It excited me. I couldn't believe the power this woman had over my cock, and maybe over my heart as well—only time would tell for that one. I wasn't about to rush into anything, but I also couldn't imagine her not being in my life.

"We should probably go," she said.

I nodded and kissed her on the cheek. "I'm going to go ahead. Wait five minutes, and then come after me." She nodded back. I kissed her deeply, taking her tongue and sucking on it.

We made out like that for a good thirty seconds, and I wished we didn't have to stop.

I left the cabin feeling happy and satisfied. I looked over my shoulder and saw her in the doorway of my cabin. I kept that image in my head all the way to the job site, not wanting to forget what she looked like standing there. Would she also look that way if we ever shared a home together? That thought definitely brought a smile to my face.

VOLUNTEERS WERE ARRIVING WEEKLY, which was a great thing for the site—the more people that showed up, the quicker things were accomplished. I was anxious to get the school completed for the sake of the children in the other building. I didn't want to hear about something awful or tragic happening because they were inside that ramshackle building. The new school was almost complete, and I could just feel the pride amongst all the workers for a job well done. When I started seeing the finished product, it was just a really good feeling to have. I had been so distracted with the work as well as with Katie that I had almost forgotten about the scandal back home.

By the time the week was over, we had a rather large team working together, and the work started to come together at a faster pace. Once the school was complete, we would band both teams together to get the hospital completed. It was a much larger project, and the finished product would really help all the local villagers. They didn't have anything that even resembled a hospital close by, and many people had died because they couldn't get to a hospital in time. After the hospital was completed, I would most likely return home. I had been there for a week already, and I would need to get back and deal with the issues of the company. At the very least I would have to deal with the deposition against me, and then maybe even a trial if the charges weren't dropped—that all depended on whether they found the person responsible for it all.

Kyle was flying into the job site that day to give me an update on what was going on back home. I was anxious to find out whether or not Kyle had gotten to the bottom of things. It was his job after all, and he had assured me that I would find out who was responsible for the order to start dumping in the ocean.

I really had been cut off from the world that past week. I had not brought my phone as I knew it would be too distracting, and there was no Wi-Fi unless I went into town—which was a rare occurrence for me. I spent all my spare time with Katie, and that was a lot better than checking social media sites or emails. Not to mention the fact that I would have driven myself nuts by checking the news every night to see what they were saying about me. The whole point of being in Africa was to get my mind off things and to fix my reputation. I didn't need to worry about any of it as long as I was in Africa. The fact that Kyle was coming to brief me on everything was enough for me for the time being.

I was on the job site when Kyle arrived. Paul had met with his plane and drove him into the site so that he could meet with me. By the time he arrived, I was enjoying lunch with Katie. We had opted to forgo the sexual lunch affair for that day, knowing that Kyle would be arriving. I didn't exactly need my right-hand man walking in on me having sex, though it was almost torturous waiting for the opportunity to touch her all over again.

By the time Kyle found me, I was covered in sweat. By this point, I was used to the heat, but it looked as if Kyle had not dressed appropriately for the sweltering heat.

"My god, man, it is hot here."

"Yeah, no kidding." I chuckled. "But trust me, you do get used to it."

"It looks like you have a killer tan to bring back to New York with you."

I smiled. "Yeah I've been spending an awful lot of time in the sun, that's for sure. I'm assuming your flight was good?"

"Yes, of course. No issue there."

I motioned to Katie. "This is Katie. She volunteers with the AIDS program, educating the children in the area. Katie, this is my right-hand man, Kyle."

"It's nice to meet you."

Kyle shook her hand with a smile on his face. It was obvious that he liked her by the way he was smiling admirably at her. I couldn't blame him, of course. She was beautiful, but I also felt a sting of jealousy when I saw Kyle talking to her.

"It's a pleasure meeting you as well." Kyle turned his attention back to me. "I need to debrief you on the situation back home. Can we speak in private?"

"Yes, of course." I glanced at Katie, noticing that she looked puzzled.

"I will catch up with you later on, okay, Katie? Enjoy the rest of your lunch."

She only nodded, not saying a word. I thought it was a little weird for her to behave that way, but I decided to let it go. I wanted to talk to Kyle and find out what was going on in New York during my absence. That, for the time being, was more important. I could speak with Katie about everything later on. I walked away with Kyle, leaving her at the table to finish her lunch.

"So, Kyle, what do you have to report? I hope you have some good news for me."

Kyle looked me over. "You look really good, man. I don't think I've ever seen you so relaxed, even after a normal vacation. I have to say Africa has done wonders for you. How's the stress level?"

"I don't have any stress here, which is exactly what I needed. It was a good suggestion to come here and lend a hand. It certainly has done me good to get away from all the stress from the accusations. I'm happy to be away from that shit for the time being." I wasn't sure what was making me happier, working at the site or spending time with Katie. Imagine if I had never gone to Africa and therefore had never met her? I couldn't even imagine such a thing. Was the whole thing fated? I wasn't sure that I believed in things like that.

"Well, I'm glad to hear it, man. You deserve a break. You don't need to worry about anything—you are going to walk away from this whole thing unscathed."

"That's what I like to hear. So tell me, what's going on? Is there any news?"

"Well, first, I came to tell you that you need to be finished your work here no later than a few weeks, and that's whether the hospital is completed or not. I know you wanted to be here to see them both completed, but you need to be back in two weeks for sure."

"Why?" I didn't like the fact that I was going to miss the completion of the hospital—there would be a real celebration after that one, and I was hoping to host it. But maybe we would get lucky and be able to finish the hospital in time as well. With both teams together, we just might be able to. Plus, I had not spoken to Katie about what was going on between us and what it would mean once I left. I couldn't imagine being gone in two weeks and leaving her here. It would be weird not having her around. Those days we basically spent every waking hour together—not to mention the hours we spent sleeping, too.

"Well, you need to appear in front of the court for the criminal charges the prosecutor is putting against you. So like I said, whether the hospital is completed or not, you need to be ready to go."

"What the fuck, Kyle! Court? I am not going to jail for the better part of my life because the Arctic Ocean was poisoned. You told me you were going to handle this."

"Ben, calm down. You don't need to get upset."

"Don't tell me I don't need to get upset, Kyle. This is my life."

"I know, and you aren't going to jail. This is all going to go away, I promise you. This will all be swept under the rug, and before you know it, everyone will be back to thinking you're an amazing man. Which you are, of course. This is just a stumbling block. We are going to be back on top."

"That would be fantastic, Kyle, and I'm expecting you to make sure that it happens." I took a deep breath, regaining my composure.

Kyle and I continued walking through the camp so that I could show him what we had been doing with the school. Neither one of us had noticed that there had been another person walking behind us the entire time.

CHAPTER SEVEN

Ben

Katie was supposed to have met me for dinner that evening, and I waited at the cabin for over an hour, wondering what was taking her so long. It was becoming clear to me that she wasn't showing up, and I couldn't have been more confused. I grew worried about her and decided to go looking for her to make sure she was all right. I found her in her own cabin. Had she forgotten our date? I found that hard to believe. She barely looked up at me as I made my way up to her porch, where she was sitting.

"Katie, did you forget dinner? I thought we were doing that together."

"Well, you were wrong about that."

Her tone startled me. She was definitely pissed; I just had no idea why. I couldn't imagine why she was suddenly so cold toward me. We were always red-hot together.

"What's wrong?"

When she looked up at me, she was glaring. Taken aback, I grew more confused by the minute. I wasn't sure what to say to her, so I remained quiet. She would eventually tell me what was up, especially if she meant to get rid of me.

Finally, she said, "How could you poison the ocean? Then you come here and you fool everyone into thinking you're a good man when really you're nothing but a fake."

I was speechless, which probably made me look guilty, but I was just thrown off by her comment. How did she know that? Had Paul finally told her? I couldn't imagine Paul doing something like that, but how else did she know?

"What are you talking about?"

"I was practically standing behind you when you were talking to Kyle. I heard everything. You both are evil."

"Katie, you're wrong. I had nothing to do with that—you don't understand."

"Isn't that convenient. How could an owner of a company not know that something like that was going on? Are you joking right now?"

"Katie, please, you have to trust me that I had no idea. I had stepped away from the company at the time to pursue other things. There were other people in charge."

"Just because you are away from the company doesn't mean you don't know what's going on."

I was astounded by what I was hearing. She was saying exactly the same things I had been beating myself up over before I went to Africa. What's worse was that she didn't believe me.

"Look, I know how it sounds, but it's not true. Kyle didn't know either, and we are trying to get to the bottom of it. I have to go to court, yes, but I'm defending myself, and the prosecutor has no proof that I did any of this. Please, Katie, you know me—I would never do this."

"It's disgusting, and I just don't believe that you had no idea."

"I have spent my whole life helping people. I would never do something like that. I came here to do good, not to trick people. Please, you know me."

"No, I think you came here to avoid a media storm or to help your precious reputation."

"I came here so that the media could see who I really am. I didn't do this, and I'm not evil or a fake. The person you know here, that's who I am. Being here has made me so happy."

She searched my eyes, and I hoped that she would just believe me, trust that I had nothing to do with disposing of the waste.

"Come back to the cabin, please."

"Don't you dare lie to me."

"Katie, I would never lie to you. You have to trust me."

She fell into my arms, and I breathed a sigh of relief. She kissed me roughly, and I grew excited with her in my arms. I walked her backward into her cabin and began to undress her quickly. She didn't share the cabin alone, and I had no idea where the other girls were, but I didn't really care.

She broke the kiss. "Ben, I don't think this is a good idea."

"We'll be quiet. Please, I need you."

THAT NIGHT, I went back to my own cabin, leaving her behind. I wanted her to be with me, but she declined, saying she needed to get some rest. When I arrived home, I realized I was also really tired and fell asleep as soon as my head hit the pillow.

When I awoke the next morning, Katie was there, sitting on the end of my bed, holding cups of coffee in her hand. I sat up, confused but pleased to find her there.

"Hi, beautiful. Thanks for bringing me coffee."

"I need to talk to you, Ben."

Her tone had me worried. "What's up?"

"I'm going home today."

I was wide-awake now. "What are you talking about?"

"I should have told you I was planning to leave, but I just wanted to enjoy our time together. I've been here for a while now, and I need to return to work. My sister told me the orders are getting out of hand."

"I don't know what I'll do without you here."

She smiled. "You'll just have to focus on that hospital now. I hope you understand that I have to leave now."

I refused to let her see that I was crushed by her leaving. I didn't understand why she was leaving—I felt like her departure was cold and too sudden. I guess we weren't on the same page after all.

"Sure, I do. I hope things go well with your orders." I was hurt that she hadn't given me any warning about her departure, but I didn't want to waste these last moments by getting in an argument.

She looked sad as she leaned over to kiss me. "Take care, Ben."

I watched her walk out of the cabin and out of my life. My heart lurched in my throat. I knew she wasn't just leaving Africa—she was leaving me too, and I knew I had to get her back.

CHAPTER EIGHT

Katie

Six Months Later

It seemed that I was always in a hurry no matter how hard I tried not to be. I felt like a chicken with my head cut off on most days, and that was never a good feeling for anyone. Every day I was filled with stress, and often I felt overloaded, but that was the life of a designer, I supposed. I loved the fashion world, and although it could be stressful at times, I wouldn't trade my life for anything.

I made my way to the café down the street to get my usual dose of caffeine to help me get through the day. I found I drank a lot of coffee, mainly because I was up late at night working on my designs, and mornings came way too fast. The café was not far from the design studio that I rented, and I always liked to bring back some cupcakes for my team—and this place made the best in the city!

I walked up to the counter and put in my order and tried as best as I could to be patient. I drummed my fingers on the countertop as I waited. I couldn't get last night's designs out of my head and wondered if they needed a bit of altering. It certainly wouldn't hurt, but I was so close to presenting them during fashion week that I didn't want to lose any time by changing things unnecessarily. Sometimes I could be a perfectionist, and that got me in hot water more often than not.

I had one very exciting thing on my schedule for the day, and just thinking about it boiled up some excitement in me. An order had come in a few weeks ago for a pop star that was looking for a particular design. The deadline was today, and I needed to have the sketches and thumbnails to the pop star that day. She needed a design for the MTV Music Awards that were coming up, and it was a true honor that I had been chosen to do the design. What more could a designer want than to see one of her dresses on a celebrity? It didn't get much better than that.

It was important that I offered the girl my best possible designs, and it had been something that weighed heavily on my mind all the time. I couldn't screw it up. This client could bring me to the next level in my career, and my heart beat faster just thinking about it.

It had been six months since I'd returned home from Africa, and it was almost as if it had never happened. It's funny how being back in the big city could make you forget certain things. The hustle and bustle of the city were nothing like the laid-back living I had found in Malawi. If I thought about it too often, I would find myself going back there mentally, and I missed it. I missed the children, the work that made me feel so fulfilled in many ways, and the people. Since I had been back, I had been working my ass off, and time just seemed to pass by me. I didn't have a lot of time to dwell on my trip.

It was important to me after seeing how things went in Africa to truly make my own dreams come true. One thing that I had learned during my trip was that life was fleeting and it went by so fast. It was important for me to chase my dreams while I was still young—I felt I owed it to my experience to do my best and to take advantage of all that I could in life.

I refused to believe that I kept myself so busy every hour of the day to try to forget something—or someone. I definitely didn't enjoy idle time in which I could just sit there and contemplate things. But there were times when I couldn't help but think about Ben and the time we had shared together. I had not spoken to Ben since I had walked away from him at his cabin. At the time I felt it was what was best for me, and I couldn't question that decision. Not now. Ben was a man who was troubled in more ways than one. I considered it a fling and nothing more. These things happened when people were away, and they generally didn't mean anything. I wanted what happened to stay in my past—there was no point in dwelling on that time.

If I were honest with myself, I would admit that maybe the crazy way I had been working lately had more to do with the fact that I was hiding unresolved feelings for Ben—which was completely stupid because we had only known each other for a short amount of time. How could I feel something for him when I'd barely spent enough time with him to get to know him? I refused to believe that I fell for a guy I had just met. Not to mention the fact that the man had never been in a serious relationship in his life—in a moment of weakness shortly after my return, I'd made the mistake of looking him up online. There were more than enough pictures of him with different women paraded around on his arm for me to understand the playboy life he was used to. It was just one more thing that made me question why I would want to shackle myself to a man like that. It was a recipe for disaster.

I had been working my ass off the past six months to disguise the fact that thinking about Ben reminded me of what it had felt like to have his hands on my body. I couldn't exactly complain though, as working my ass off had really paid off and the company I started had grown significantly. Things were going great, business-wise—I had a great team, and they worked just as hard as I did in making sure my designs were realized. At first, I had been doing all the work myself, and now I had people to whom I could delegate those tasks. It was a liberating feeling, and I couldn't be happier with the position I was in.

That was the upside to life after Ben. The downside was that I often found myself standing in a coffee line with a zombie expression across my face. I would be laughing, however, if the pop star loved my design and wore it to the show. The pop star could make a garbage bag look good, so if she wore my design it was likely that more orders would just keep piling in.

I smiled at the barista as he handed me the trays of coffee and cupcakes. My team would need it just as much as I did, and I liked taking care of a hardworking team. Getting coffee gave me the same feeling as when I was helping people in Africa—I just liked making people happy. It made my life so much more fulfilling.

When I stepped outside, the sun was beating down so brightly that I had to stop for a moment to take it in. I rarely stopped and took a breath, yet there I was standing in the middle of the sidewalk, just forcing myself to relax and enjoy the sun for a moment. The rays felt good against my skin, and this was one of the rare moments where I was transported back to Africa.

I loved my life—there wasn't a bad thing about it. I should be grateful. I also should consider slowing down so I didn't burn out. There were people in the world dying, so to be stressed about whether my designs would sell or not was a silly thing. After all, life went on—it always did. My future looked bright and successful, so what was I stressing out about? I needed to start living my life as if every day was my last.

I headed toward my office with a new lightness to my step, thinking about how great the day was going to be. I opened the doors to the brightly lit studio. One of the interns made a beeline for me and snatched the trays from my hands.

"Thanks, Becky. It wasn't easy getting those here. I'm surprised I didn't drop them."

"Yeah, I know what you mean. I've definitely done something like that myself." Becky brought around the coffee to people and set out the cupcakes for whoever chose to come for them. They would be gone in twenty minutes, I could guarantee it.

"Something came for you today."

"What is it?"

"No idea. But it looks fancy."

I laughed. "I can't imagine what it is. Unless the pop star is trying to inspire me to create faster."

"I have no idea who it's from."

"How mysterious." I couldn't imagine who the package would be from—I hadn't ordered anything lately. I followed Becky to my office, where a box sat on my desk. We both looked down at it, but I still couldn't determine where it came from. The package was wrapped in paper that could only be described as luxurious, which only further puzzled me.

"I have to tell you, Katie, it looks like it could be a romantic gift."

"What? Do you think?"

"Just unwrap it, for goodness' sake. The suspense is killing me."

"Okay, hold on," I laughed. I quickly unwrapped the mysterious package to find a gorgeous blue dress sitting there with a diamond necklace on top.

"Oh my god."

"Hey, there's a letter in there," whispered Becky.

"Where?"

"Right there!" Becky was practically yelling at me.

I chuckled. "Easy there, girl, I didn't see it."

Becky handed me the letter, and I turned it over to see if there was a name. There wasn't. I quickly opened the letter to find directions to the hottest French restaurant in town. I was to wear the dress and necklace when I went there tonight at seven.

"Wow. That is so romantic."

"I have no idea what is going on right now," I muttered.

"It has to be Matt."

"Really, you think so?" The thought of Matt sending me a package like this made me grow warm all over. I'd only been seeing him for a short time, but things were progressing nicely.

"Of course—who else could it be? He sent you those flowers the other day too. He's on a roll."

"Yeah, but flowers are one thing—this is something else entirely."

"Sure, but the guy is loaded. It's not like he can't afford it."

I stared down at the letter, wondering. It would be a sweet gesture, but it just seemed too soon for two people who had just started to get to know one another. But maybe Matt was trying to woo me on an extreme level.

"What should I do?"

"You should definitely go."

"Really? I don't know."

"Are you crazy, Katie? If a guy did something like that for me, I would already be on my way over even if I was like ten hours early."

I laughed. "Yeah, but that's assuming you think it's Matt. It could be a stalker waiting at that table for me. Super creepy."

"Come on. You can't be serious."

"Well, it's not like I haven't been splashed all over the papers lately. It could be anyone that sent this. To be honest, if it was Matt, I think it would say so."

"Whoa, Katie, you are way over-thinking this one. Yes, it's only been a week since you met Matt, but he's been contacting you nonstop ever since. He could just be doing a romantic gesture."

I nodded. "Yeah, I guess you're right. Maybe I am over-reacting."

"Well, I'll leave you to it. I need to drink my coffee and get back to work. I'm swamped."

"Yes, please do. You really help keep things afloat."

I sat down at my desk and started to sift through some paperwork. I kept looking up at the box, unable to concentrate. Who sent that beautiful dress? I picked up the letter again, reading it over. I then touched the fabric of the dress. There was one thing I could tell for sure—it was expensive material, and the necklace was on a whole other level entirely. Becky had been right about one thing, the package had been fancy. I just wasn't sure Matt was behind it.

Thinking about Matt always brought a smile to my face. I really liked the guy, but I didn't think he would make such a grand gesture, especially so soon. So far we always had a great time together, so maybe I was underestimating his attraction to me. Maybe he was all about the grand gesture.

I met Matt while attending an AIDS gala fundraiser. Since leaving Africa, I wanted to be more involved in the cause. I may not be building schools or teaching students, but I still wanted to be part of the cause and lend a hand where I could now that I was home. I had allowed one of my dresses to be auctioned off for the cause, and it had sold for almost $10,000. That was nothing to sneeze at. I ended up meeting Matt because he had been seated at the same table as I was. He was tall, dark, and hard all over—very hard to resist. He was a little older than I was, but I didn't mind at all. He owned one of the major football teams in the area and was quite successful. I had a hard time not thinking about him.

We had spent the better part of the evening talking and laughing together. Later on that night, the organizer had confessed that Matt had asked to sit at my table. I had been surprised but deeply flattered. I had never met a kinder and more thoughtful man, and spending time with him had been a real treat. I couldn't have had more fun that night, and I doubted that I would have had as good a time had he not been there to entertain me.

He had asked me out that night, and we had dinner the next evening. We'd been talking nonstop ever since. After that first date, I had been sure that there was a reason that Matt had been brought into my life. I could really believe that he might be the one. Or was I talking crazy as well? We had only met a week ago, but then this box arrived. What did it mean?

Matt was a sexy, successful, and kind man—I should snap him up while I could. Although he was one hell of a sexy guy, we had yet to sleep together. Not that I wanted to rush things—I was fine with how things were going.

I made my decision. I was going to go to the restaurant to meet that mystery man.

CHAPTER NINE

Katie

I drank a glass of wine as I got ready for my mystery date. It was a good way to relax before I went to meet whoever was waiting for me. It was probably Matt—I mean, who else would send such an extravagant gift?

Overall the day had gone marvelously well. The sketches had been completed on time and sent over to the pop star for approval. Just sending the sketches had been so exciting. I was really doing it—doing what I loved and making strides toward realizing my dreams. At least the stress of those sketches was a thing of the past. Now I just had to wait for the final approval and the dress could be made.

I looked in the mirror and spun around. The dress was tight-fitting and showed off my curves. Whoever bought the dress knew my size and knew what I liked because I looked like a fox in it. It made me wonder how on earth Matt would know my size so well when he had never even seen me naked. Had he just guessed? I slipped on the diamond necklace and attached the clasp, feeling the heaviness of the necklace against my chest.

I looked in the mirror again and smiled. Damn, I looked good. That necklace was stunning, and it complemented the dress so well. I couldn't wait to get to the restaurant and show Matt what I looked like in the items he had so carefully picked out for me. He would be thrilled—the look on his face alone would be priceless. I decided to put on my sexiest pair of lace panties that evening, just in case he felt inspired after he saw me. If he did feel so inspired, he would get a night that he wouldn't soon forget.

I decided it was best to take a cab to the restaurant since I wasn't entirely sure what would be happening afterward. If nothing happened it would take nothing to cab back home. I didn't really want to worry about driving if I was having a few drinks either.

When I arrived, I stepped into the high-class restaurant and looked toward the host. My heart was beating in my chest like crazy. It was the kind of restaurant that took months to get a reservation, and it had been some time since I had been there. Whoever sent the dress definitely had some connections.

The host approached me, and I announced that I was meeting an unknown visitor. The hostess took my name and smiled as she led the way to my table. I tried to steady my heart, but it was raging out of control and there was nothing that I could do about it. I was being seated out on the terrace, and when I approached the table, there was no one there yet. The plot thickened even more. They were literally the best seats in the house, looking out into the evening stars. It took my breath away.

I looked around the restaurant to see if I could see Matt coming in. I wanted to be all smiles for him. What I did not expect was to see Ben walking toward me. My mouth hit the floor, and not in a flattering way. He had a shit-eating grin on his face, and suddenly everything was coming into focus. Shit, what was he doing there?

I had forgotten just how handsome Ben actually was, but it all came screaming back as he approached me. I hadn't seen him since Africa, and seeing Ben in front of me then had me reliving every moment we spent together in my head. He wasn't even that close to me, and yet my body temperature rose just at the sight of him. He was, after all, still the only man that had ever given me an orgasm.

I shook it off. I couldn't believe I could still feel that way about him after so long. It had been six months, and yet it felt like it was yesterday. It felt like he had just put his hands on me for the first time. How was that possible? For him to have that kind of control over my body after all that time? I blushed at the thought of everything he'd made me feel. He was still smiling at me, and it was causing an ache inside.

"You look as beautiful as the day I met you. That is quite the dress."

I narrowed my eyes at him. "Ben, what the hell are you doing here?"

"Should I be offended that you weren't expecting me?"

Oh no, was the package from him? Is that what he was implying? I refused to give him any more of a reaction than a smile. I wasn't going to bring Matt into this mess. I couldn't believe he was standing there before me, but I should have known. It would have been too soon for Matt to have pulled such an extravagant gesture on me. I just hadn't expected to ever hear from Ben again.

"Did you really expect me to give up on you that easily? You are all I've thought about for the past six months."

"Well, you sure know how to mark your territory, don't you?"

He took a seat across from me, and my nervousness swelled. I had expected Matt to be there across from me, and instead I had received a blast from my past. Would Matt be upset to know I was having dinner with an old flame? No, it was much too soon for him to feel that kind of possessiveness toward me. He would have no right to be upset. We weren't exclusive and had never even had a conversation even close to that.

I couldn't help but feel torn. I knew that I still had some unresolved feelings for Ben, and yet I really liked Matt. There was the potential for something to be there between us. In fact, I had been having the kind of thoughts that included a white dress and baby clothing. I was in no rush for any of those things, of course, but it was just the kind of thoughts girls had when they met a guy they really liked. I could be happy with a man like Matt—he was the perfect family man.

But there was no denying the incredible chemistry that came with spending time with Ben—we were electric together. I just had no idea if there was a future with Ben. Our time together in Malawi had been incredible, right up until it wasn't. I still couldn't get over the fact that he had hidden something so huge from me while we were together, and I didn't know if I could trust him. Plus, knowing about his past with women, I couldn't be certain if he would be there from one day to the next.

"Tell me, Katie, how have you been these past few months?" His smile warmed me immediately.

"Things are great. My company is on fire right now. A celeb asked me to design a dress, so that's exciting."

"Good for you, I'm happy to hear it. I can't say I'm surprised at all though. You are one hell of a smart woman."

I smiled at him. I was proud of my accomplishments and a little pleased that he was as well. I always felt at ease with Ben; we had a level of comfort that was hard to attain with most people without spending many years with them.

As we ordered drinks and then dinner, the time between us flew. We talked like old friends and didn't shut up for hours. It was like I had been starving before he showed up, and he brought me sustenance just by being in my presence.

We eventually got around to discussing Africa and what went on there after I had left. The experience had changed Ben for the better, and I could see that when he spoke of his experience there. We also discussed his upcoming trial and what he hoped to do about it.

The phone rang then, breaking through my reverie. Thinking it was my design team looking for me I flipped my phone over and saw that it was Matt calling. I sent the call to voice mail and flipped the phone back over. I couldn't talk to Matt while I was having dinner with another man. It would have been disrespectful to both of them.

I looked up to see Ben watching me intently. "Important call?" he said with a glint in his eyes.

"Don't worry about who's calling me, Ben."

The phone rang again, startling me, and we both laughed. "If you need to take a call, Katie, you can do so."

"No, it's okay." I laughed. "I'm sorry."

"Well, check who it is and make sure it's not important."

I flipped the phone over, and this time it was my design team. Becky was calling and I clicked on the call immediately. There was so much chattering going on that I could barely understand what she was saying.

"Becky, calm down. I can hardly hear you."

I paused as I listened to Becky, who continued on in a calmer voice. "Oh my god! That's incredible." I was laughing and it felt great. I clicked off the call and beamed at Ben.

"Must have been good news."

"Oh, great news. That celebrity I was telling you about, she loved the design and she wants the dress."

"Congratulations, Katie. You certainly deserve it." He got up from his chair and circled toward me. He pulled me out of my chair and into his arms for a hug, and my body hummed with the connection to him. When we parted, I looked up into his eyes and it was just like that first night we were together. I kissed him right there in the middle of the restaurant, and he returned my kiss just as fervently.

"Come to my hotel room," he whispered against my neck. "I have one upstairs."

I wondered if he had planned the whole thing, but I realized I didn't care. I nodded.

CHAPTER TEN

Katie

We made our way up the elevator to the penthouse suite without a word spoken between us. Once inside the suite, Ben scooped me into his arms and carried me to his room, where he lay me down on the bed.

My mind raced as I looked up at his eyes filled with lust. Was it possible that my heart was beating even more furiously? I thought it was going to burst through my rib cage and come through my chest. Thump, thump, thump—oh god, I might even pass out. I'd never felt so brazen with anyone else, but there was just something about him. He made me want to be naughty. Knowing Ben wanted nothing more than to please me in as many ways as possible made me grow warm all over. I was becoming incredibly horny as his tongue continued to play with mine.

He just stared at me, and I could tell he was feeling the same way that I was. He wanted me and I remembered what it had been like between us. God, that turned me on so much. What was he about to do to me?

"So, what should we do first?" I said with a wink.

He flashed me a devilish grin that made me warm all over. "I'm going to make you feel really good, Katie, by doing dirty things to you."

I gasped. Before Ben, no one had ever talked that way to me before, and I'd had some pretty darn good sex in my day—even if it hadn't always come with a side of orgasm. Why had no one done it before? It hadn't even occurred to me before being with Ben that I would be so into dirty talk, but I certainly liked it now. From the first night we'd had sex, Ben had talked to me in that manner, and it was intoxicating.

He leaned in and slipped his hand around my neck, pulling me in to him as his mouth claimed mine. He tasted sweet and alluring. His mouth was hot to the touch, and I almost moaned as his lips caressed mine. He kissed me softly at first, and then his kisses became more fevered, as if he needed my mouth on his. His tongue slipped into my mouth, and I claimed it. I sucked him slowly, tasting him before I pulled away. He pulled me in again, showing me that he was not finished kissing me. His tongue found mine again, and our kisses grew more passionate. His hand found my breast, and he kneaded it softly. He began unzipping the dress and tossed it aside. He stopped kissing me momentarily to look down at my breasts that were dying to be released from my bra.

"You are beautiful," he said with a smile.

I smiled, though all I could think about was what he looked like naked. He unclasped my bra and pushed me back until I was pushed up against the bed. His mouth found my nipple, and he sucked, nipped, and licked it. The sensations racing through my body were making my lace panties wet. I moaned softly as Ben replaced his mouth with his fingers and pulled on my nipple, causing an ache between my legs. I liked it and couldn't help the way my body was reacting. He continued playing with my nipples, making me moan as pleasure built up in my body. I reached down with my hand and massaged the front of his pants. I could feel his hard cock pushing against his pants.

He smiled down at me. "Do you want it? Do you want it in your mouth?"

I nodded, still speechless at the things that came out of his mouth. I felt wanton around him, like I would do just about anything for pleasure—to have him please my body, to give me what I wanted.

He undid the button on his pants and pulled the zipper down. He brought his pants down to his knees and slid his underwear down with them. His hard cock bounced before me now, free from his underwear. He was so big—the sight was always breathtaking to me, and I had forgotten how impressive he was in the flesh. He stood in front of me, his cock in my face. I took his cock into my mouth and sucked on it. His eyes closed above me, and I sucked hard while I massaged his balls. My tongue began to swirl against his shaft and then around his tip. He moaned with eagerness, and I sucked him even harder.

"Oh god, you're good at this."

I took his cock deeper into my mouth until it hit the back of my throat. I moved up and down rhythmically until I moved fluidly with him in my mouth.

His moans excited me, and I felt my pussy become even wetter. He pulled his cock out of my mouth and finished undressing.

"Mmm, you look good. Maybe good enough to eat."

I didn't hesitate to lean back on the bed and spread my legs. I wanted him between my legs. I wanted him to lick my pussy.

He dropped down before me and licked my pussy slowly, as if he was savoring my taste. It felt incredible as his tongue licked the sides of my opening, causing a tingle to run through my body. He took my clit into his mouth and sucked on it, making me moan loudly as my pussy dripped.

"Oh god... oh god..." I could hardly catch my breath, it felt so good.

He looked up and smiled. "Does that feel good, sweetheart?"

"Oh god yes, it feels incredible."

My pussy was dripping, and he was licking it up, tasting every inch of me. I felt the buildup coming, that sweet sensation that only he had been able to give me. I was going to cum right there in his penthouse suite.

"Oh god... oh wow—I'm going to cum."

He was sucking on my clit when he buried a finger inside my pussy and started pumping away. It was too much—too much all at once, and I cried out softly as I had an orgasm so delicious that I wanted even more.

"How was that?" His cocky grin said he knew exactly how it was.

I just grinned back with desire written all over my face.

"Let me sit down, baby. I want you to sit on my cock and ride it."

I grinned, loving the sound of his words. He lay down on the bed, and I got into position with my back facing him, and plunged myself onto his cock. He was pushed right up against my G-spot in that position and the feeling made me just about lose my mind.

I was rendered speechless, and I started moving slowly. He felt fantastic, and I rode his smooth cock even harder. He was moaning softly as well, and it made me want to give him as much pleasure as I was receiving.

"Mmmm, you're such a sexy girl. You feel delicious. You ride my cock good, baby."

I moaned. His voice, his words, his cock were driving me

mad. And just when I thought it couldn't get any better, he reached around and started playing with my clit. It was almost too much to bear—I couldn't get enough. I was moaning softly, wanting to beg for more but already feeling so possessed by him. My pussy was so wet. He was driving me wild.

"Just relax, sweetheart."

I gasped as pleasure coursed through me. I continued pumping onto his cock as an orgasm took hold of me once again. "Oh god, Ben, oh god that feels so good." I whispered my yearnings to him.

"I want to put my cock in you and fuck you. It's my turn."

I lifted myself off his cock and waited to see what he had in mind.

His cock—oh god. Looking at his size made shock waves course through me. I wanted to be fucked by him desperately.

I couldn't believe all that was happening. It was hard to believe I was in that situation, there with Ben, whom I hadn't seen in months, but loving every moment with him. He made my body throb until I wanted to beg him to release me from that feeling. I needed him to fuck me so that I would get the release that I craved, the release that I so deserved. I was already two orgasms in, but I wasn't satisfied yet. I wanted to be fucked over and over again by that man. This was the kind of therapy one needed after a tough day at the office—screw therapy, or wine, or hot baths. The way to feel better was to be fucked properly.

He got up from the bed and pushed me back down on it. When he pushed my legs up over my head, my eyes widened. Thank god I was flexible.

I did as I was told, my body weakened from pleasure. I was lying on my back, my legs spread before him and above him.

"Touch yourself for me."

My eyes popped open. I shook my head. "I can't."

"Yes, you can. I want to see you please yourself—it turns me on. Then I'm going to slide inside that wet pussy of yours and fuck you really good."

Nervousness swelled inside my stomach. I had masturbated before, obviously, but never in front of anyone. So I did what any sane woman would do, and I spread my legs and slid my fingers through the wetness that was all over my pussy. I swirled it around before moving up to my clit, massaging it with my finger. I ground into it, closing my eyes as I enjoyed my own touch.

I was sure my face was a bright crimson, but he didn't say a thing. In fact, when I opened my eyes he was staring down at me, mesmerized by what I was doing. He looked up at me with fire in his eyes, and the look on his face made me feel incredible, like I was completely in control of his pleasure. I loved the feeling of controlling his lust, and I inserted two fingers into my pussy and moaned as they went in deep. I finger-fucked myself in front of him, watching him as a slow smile formed on his face.

"That is so hot."

I moaned as I pleasured myself, taking my fingers out and swirling my juices around my clit. My body was throbbing all over, and I desperately wanted to be fucked by that point.

"Please?"

"Please what, darling? Do you want some help?"

"I want you."

"Then you can have me." He positioned himself in the missionary position and put my legs up over my head again. He entered me slowly, and I gasped with how deep he went.

"Oh yes, this is nice. You're nice and tight, baby. God your pussy feels so good." The level of deepness in that position was crazy good.

I leaned my head back, delirious with pleasure. He fit inside me perfectly, and I got a wave of pleasure every time he moved inside of me. He began pumping me a little faster, and I moaned so loudly the room below us must have heard. His cock was perfect, and with the position we were in, he was perfectly placed to hit my G-spot. My body built up once again, and I knew that he was going to make me cum soon.

"Cum for me, baby. I can see it on your face. Cum all over my cock."

I exploded then, doing as he asked, screaming. I was spent and yet he kept fucking me slowly. He pulled out, and I rolled onto my stomach, my ass high in the air. This was my favorite position with him

"You have such a nice ass. You should see this glorious view that I have."

He slid inside my pussy hard. I cried out as pleasure overtook my body yet again. I moaned, enjoying every inch of his cock as he pounded me over and over again. He leaned down toward me and spanked my ass. I cried out, realizing I had never experienced anything so sexy in my entire life. He pumped into me harder, waves of pleasure rolling off me. I looked over my shoulder and smiled up at him, stifling my moans as best I could as another orgasm ripped through me. I was having multiple orgasms with this man—how could I not miss being with him?

"You have a really nice pussy, Katie. I like fucking you."

I moaned, loving the way he was making me feel, and loving even more the way he talked to me.

He pulled out again and turned me over. He slid his fingers into my pussy and finger-fucked me for a bit. He was making me wet all over again, although at that point I was pretty soaked from all the fucking. "I want you back on my cock, baby. Will you sit on me again and ride me good?"

"You bet your ass I will."

He lay back down, and I positioned myself so that I had my back to him again, and slid his cock inside me.

"There we go, darling—we're going to go easy. That feels good, doesn't it?" I moaned in agreement.

"Okay, here we go. Just stay relaxed, don't tense up."

I could hardly believe myself at that moment. What had ever possessed me to do such a thing, getting together with Ben again? God, I had wanted him so badly—I still did. I was so sexually satisfied, yet so horny still—I would have let him do just about anything to me. I was aching inside with want for him.

I rode Ben's cock, feeling the delicious sensations spread all over my body.

"Just relax, sweetheart, you're tensing up. I can feel you hugging my cock."

I hadn't realized that I was holding my breath, so I did as he said. As I pushed onto him a little more, I tried to relax and allowed it to happen. He certainly felt huge when he was going in on this end. I felt full with him in my pussy, but I loved every moment of it. He then began to move his hips and meet my thrusts as I slid down onto his cock. He was trying to allow me to get used to having more of him inside of me. I moaned as he picked up the pace, his smooth cock gliding in and out.

"Are you okay, Katie?"

"Yes," I whispered.

"Does it feel good?"

"God yes. I love learning new positions with you."

The thought of having a variety of positions available to me had never occurred to me, but it sounded like a hot idea. That was one of the things that I liked most about sex with Ben—it was always new. Riding him, he felt humongous inside me. He rocked into me slowly, continuing to meet my thrusts. I started rocking into him faster, letting the waves of pleasure crash into me repeatedly, never stopping for a break between thrusts.

"Oh god," I moaned.

He reached around and felt for my pussy. He rubbed against

my moist clit, giving me some added pleasure while he moved his cock inside of me.

"Okay, baby, I want you to fuck me good."

I thought I would lose my mind with the words coming out of his mouth. He was sexy and experienced, and he was showing me a world I had never thought existed. Or one that I at least never imagined I would venture into. The sex had been good when we were together in Africa, but this was something more.

The whole length of his cock slowly pushed inside me, causing me to let out a slow and powerful moan. There were so many different feelings and sensations going through my body at that moment. I was lost in a sea of pleasure, and I wanted to let go of another orgasm.

"I want more."

I heard him chuckle, and he started pumping me hard as I thrust onto him. I was delirious with the pleasure he was giving me—I needed it, needed him.

I was dripping wet, and I felt a buildup once again. I couldn't believe I was about to cum again. God, the thought was just too delicious.

"Ben, it feels good. It really does feel so good."

"I know, baby. It's amazing, isn't it?"

"Yes," I gasped. "I'm coming again."

My whole body shuddered as I came and he continued pumping inside of me. He was glorious—all of it was so incredible. The best sex of my life was happening in that hotel suite. Before the aftershocks had even finished I felt myself build up for another orgasm—I was so sensitive from all the orgasms that the smallest touch set me off. Shudders ripped through my body, causing me to scream his name.

"Oh Katie, I'm ready too, baby. I'm going to fill up your pussy with my cum."

I moaned, loving how sexy he was with his dirty talk. He spilled inside of me and collapsed back onto the bed.

I slid slowly off his cock, and I knew for certain that I was going to be very sore the next day. It had all been worth it. I leaned toward the end table where a box of Kleenex stood and pulled out some tissues. I cleaned myself off as best I could and slipped into my panties. I then put on my dress as I watched him rummaging around for his clothes that had fallen to the floor. Finding them, he quickly slipped into underwear and dress pants, pulling his shirt over his head.

Everything was a little more rumpled than I would have liked, but hopefully no one would notice as I left the hotel. I couldn't wipe the grin off my face though. My hands shook from the toll the orgasms had taken on my body—a part of me couldn't believe I was even able to stand. Ben was watching me get dressed, and when I looked up at him, he smiled. He had a stunner of a smile, and the look of him made me want to start all over again. Would I ever be able to get enough of that man, or was it always going to be this way? God, I hoped it was.

I knew he wanted me to spend the night, but I wasn't going to do that. He came to me and kissed me softly on the lips.

"Come to Paris with me for a couple of days."

I laughed. "I can't. I have work."

"You can take a few days off to celebrate the new client you have."

"No, I need to actually work on her dress now."

"Do it on Monday."

A small smile played on my face.

11

CHAPTER ELEVEN

Katie

The last day in Paris was a sad one for me. The city was just so beautiful that I couldn't get over it. I couldn't even believe I had allowed Ben to take me there. I had so much work waiting for me back home, but it had only been for a few days, so really no harm was done. I didn't tell my design team the truth about where I was going because I didn't want them to know that I had just skipped town with an old flame, especially since some of them knew about Matt. What a complication that was. I didn't even know myself what I was doing, so having to try to explain it to someone else would be complicated and possibly embarrassing as well.

I had called Matt before I left for Paris to let him know I would be out of town for a few days. I told him we would need to talk when I returned. One way or another, I needed to make a decision and decide what man I wanted in my life—and that was no easy decision considering the two men.

Ben and I had flown to Paris almost immediately, taking advantage of his private jet. I loved Paris. Not only was it beautiful, but it was also the fashion capital of the world. I loved shopping there; they always had such unique collections.

We had only been there for a few days, and the first one didn't really count because we never left the room once—or even the bed. I had been terribly sore because of it, but it had all been worth it. The two of us weren't big on sightseeing, so we spent most of our time lounging on the beach or in the pool on the balcony of Ben's suite. It was luxurious and I loved the chance to soak up some heat before I returned home. It had been a truly relaxing time away.

It wasn't all beach time though. I had done a massive amount of shopping, but what girl wouldn't? I didn't just purchase clothing; I bought yards of fabric for my designs and had them shipped back home. It was all on Ben's dime too; he spoiled me rotten while we were away.

We were lounging by the pool sipping champagne, and I couldn't remember a time that I felt happier about my life. Everything was going to plan. Ben got up to check his messages, and I continued to sip on the decadent wine. I refused to check messages because listening to any of them would have had me back on the jet and returning home. I had a hard time leaving my company in the hands of others, and if something went wrong, I wanted to be there. So I just made sure to check in periodically through text message.

When I grabbed my phone to send my check-in message, I noticed that Matt had sent me two texts. They were simple messages, asking how my trip was coming along. I quickly sent him a text asking if he wanted to have dinner with me when I returned to the city. I knew I needed to have a talk with him.

When I turned from my phone, I found Ben standing behind me. He didn't look happy to find me on my phone, which I found odd since he regularly checked in with his office.

"I ordered us in some food so we could spend our last night relaxing. I hope that's okay with you."

"Sure, of course."

"Was that work?" He nodded toward my phone.

"They are just anxious to get me back in the office, that's all. I can't blame them. Like I said, it's a busy time for us."

Ben was watching me intently, and I wondered if he believed me. Finally, he smiled and leaned in for a kiss. He claimed my tongue and roughly squeezed my breasts. I moaned and started rubbing his cock through his shorts, the way I knew he liked. We had taken a day off sex because I had been so sore, but I was ready to take him in again. In fact, it was all I could think about at that moment.

Our hands were everywhere while our tongues mingled, and I felt myself grow wet with yearning. I wanted him inside me immediately.

"Fuck me, Ben, right now." I gave him a cheeky grin. "That is, if you can catch me."

I peeled off my bikini top and bottom and ran to the pool and jumped in. I giggled as I reached the surface and saw that he was plunging in after me. I swam to the shallow end and waited by the edge of the pool. He quickly found me, pushing me up against the wall. His mouth met mine eagerly, and I moaned loudly, aching all over my body. I wrapped my legs around his waist, and he entered me hard, pumping into me fast. My body exploded with pleasure, and I wrapped my legs around him tighter. He bit into my neck, making me cry out with pleasure.

"Oh, Ben, your cock feels so good."

"You're all mine baby."

"Oh, it feels so good."

He plunged deep inside me, over and over until I came,

arching my back into the edge of the pool. He continued to pump inside me, harder still, until he came too.

Exhausted, I leaned into his neck and hugged him with my arms. He made me feel incredible—we had an undeniable chemistry that just made our sex life so much better.

He pulled apart from me. "Let's go see if the food is here," he said. His grin made me laugh, and I climbed out of the pool with him. As I toweled myself dry, I watched as he went back into the room to check on the room service. I felt so satisfied I could have fallen asleep right then and there.

I returned to the room and noticed my phone was buzzing. When I went to check it, I found that Matt had responded. I suddenly felt guilty for being there with Ben when Matt was so into me. But I wasn't doing anything wrong—I had never slept with Matt, and we were nowhere near being exclusive. I just wanted to make sure I was making the best decision for myself.

The last thing I had expected when I started talking to Matt was that Ben would walk back into my life. I had assumed it was over between us when I had left Africa. Since coming back in my life, Ben had made some huge romantic gestures that I just couldn't ignore. I read Matt's message, noting that he agreed to dinner and offered to pick me up. I put my phone away and returned to Ben.

WE DINED on lobster and salads while we lay in bed talking about everything under the sun. We were talking about the future and what that meant for each of us. It was nice for me to catch up with Ben; I hadn't realized how much I had missed him until now. Ben had ordered in strawberries and champagne, and I dined on them while we talked. We always laughed so easily together. That was one thing that was never forced between us—we always had such a good time together.

I had never struggled to find good men in my life though. Some of my friends had some incredible disaster stories, and yet I never did. I regularly met good men who treated me well—in that way, I was very blessed. Falling in love was a pretty big deal for me, and being happy as well. If I had those things, then the rest was just a bonus for me. But that was what everyone wanted, right? To be happy and fall in love with an incredible person?

As we lay side by side on the bed, I nuzzled up next to him and sipped my champagne. Now was as good as any time to feel him out about the future of our relationship. I needed to make a decision about my life, and knowing where Ben's head was at would be a great help.

"So Ben, what are we doing here?"

"What do you mean?"

I chuckled. "I'm asking you if you see this—I mean us—going anywhere."

"Oh man, are we having the talk? Really?"

Surprised, I looked up at him, confused by his tone. "What's going on, Ben? Is there a problem with discussing us?"

"Well, I'm just a little surprised you're bringing it up right now. We're having a good time. Why do we have to define it right now?"

My stomach felt like there was a piece of lead inside of it. I wasn't sure if I should continue the talk; it was already going so poorly as it was. "I hope you're joking."

"Well, I didn't mean it that way."

"Okay, so explain yourself. How did you mean it?"

He looked down at me, and I didn't see anything good in his face. I was a little shocked because I believed that all his grand gestures had really meant something. But it looked as if his playboy ways had not disappeared, and now I was paying the price for it. I had been stupid to think that he wanted more than another roll in the hay.

"I just have a lot going on right now, especially with the trial coming up. I'm not even sure what's going on with that yet. I don't think it's a good time to get serious with anyone. I love spending time with you, Katie, don't get me wrong. It's just I don't see any reason why we need to rush things. I hope that doesn't upset you."

I wasn't sure how to take his answer at all. It wasn't like I was expecting to be engaged or anything like that, but I doubted that either of our lives was so hectic that an exclusive relationship was out of the question. The fact that he had come looking for me at all... It should have meant something, and it turned out that it was just him showing off and nothing more. All I could do was stare at him, speechless. I didn't have any words to explain to him how I was feeling. He looked slightly alarmed, probably because he realized I didn't like a thing coming out of his mouth.

"Sweetheart, I'm not trying to upset you. It's not that I don't want more, because I do. I just don't see why we can't take things slow for now. I've never been in a long-term relationship before, and it's a lot to take in."

"Seriously, how old are you?"

His mouth dropped open. "What?"

"The way you're talking it's like you're some college student not wanting to make a commitment to his college gal. It's ridiculous that you're afraid of commitment at your age." The words stung him, but I didn't care. It was ridiculous that I even had to hear these things, and I had a sudden urge to slap him across the face. I had given him more than my body on that trip—I had allowed him inside my heart, and for what? So that we could take it slow because it was a lot for him to take in?

I wasn't sure why I had allowed myself to get close to him

again. Why? So I could be hurt all over again? I should have left Ben in the past where he belonged.

"It's clear to me that we are not on the same page and we're looking for different things. Had I known how you felt, I wouldn't have come to Paris with you. I thought when you came looking for me that it meant something special."

"It was special. What exactly do you want here? A ring?"

His words stung like a slap, and I felt my blood boiling. How dare he treat me as if I had unreasonable expectations?

"Don't let your ego get too out of control there, Ben. I wasn't looking for a ring. I just thought that I mattered to you."

He was speechless and I felt a small victory.

"I no longer feel comfortable spending the night with you. Can you arrange for another room?"

"Are you serious? Katie, please."

"Don't, Ben. Just make the arrangements."

"Katie, don't you think you might be overreacting a little bit? Come on."

"It's pretty simple. We want different things. I'm sorry I don't want to continue seeing you after tonight. You may want to take things slow, but I'm ready for something with some staying power."

His mouth formed a thin line, and he got up to make a call to the front desk. I started packing my things so I wouldn't have to come and collect them the next morning. I quickly dressed in shorts and a T-shirt, knowing someone would be arriving to collect my bags. I felt sad inside but didn't know what else to do. I wanted more and he wasn't ready for it.

He didn't say a word to me as I packed, and I knew the thought of me sleeping apart from him was eating him up inside. I knew the very thought probably made him insane.

"I'll meet you in the lobby in the morning so we can catch our flight," I said as I walked toward the door.

He nodded just as the elevator opened into the penthouse. An attendant came in and collected my things. I took one more look at Ben before heading to my new room. Changing rooms, however, didn't make anything any easier. I didn't sleep a wink that night.

BACK IN NEW YORK, I was unpacking from my trip, feeling very uneasy about everything. It was important for me to have everything unpacked before I began my evening, as I hated coming back to disorganization. I had dinner plans with Matt, and I was torn up about it, confusion mixing my thoughts up into a mess.

Originally I had planned on letting Matt down easy while I worked on a future with Ben, but that had crashed and burned with very little warning. I didn't understand how I could have been so wrong about Ben, that I had read the situation so wrong. I thought he'd returned for me because he couldn't live without me, but that hadn't been the case at all. Nothing had turned out the way I'd envisioned it. I couldn't believe he'd gone to so much trouble just to have a little fun. But I supposed for a billionaire, it probably didn't seem like such a big deal to whisk a girl off to Paris or send her expensive presents. I had looked too much into it, and that was my own fault. I had misunderstood what he wanted from me, and it made me feel like a fool.

Sleeping apart from Ben that final night had been devastating. The few days we'd spent together had been incredible, and I didn't understand why he didn't want more from me. I wasn't sure if I was being unreasonable or if he was. I had cried myself to sleep that night wondering if I was making a big mistake. In the end, I had expected him to come looking for me, to apologize, and he never came. It was his decision, and I had to accept that and move on.

That wasn't where the torture had ended, unfortunately. I

had to see him the next day and fly back home with him. It wasn't a short flight either, and it had been incredibly awkward having him there with me. Neither of us spoke to each other the entire time. Ben clearly had a lot on his mind, but I would have been okay to speak to him and remain civil. It appeared as if he didn't want anything to do with me after I had walked out on him the night before. I guess it really had been just about sex for him.

Either way, he was upset with me, and I didn't think that I had done anything wrong. I just wanted something more for my future, and he wasn't willing to give that to me—how else should I have reacted? When we did finally land at the airport, there were two limos waiting instead of one, and we went our separate ways without another word to each other. I cried again on the way home, feeling more lost than ever.

Since then I had been a jumbled mess and even considered canceling my dinner date with Matt. I wasn't really in the right state of mind to see anyone or make a decent decision. In the end, however, I decided against canceling on him since I hadn't been very fair to him recently. I had no intention of having sex with him, but I needed to talk to him and see how I felt around him.

When the time came to go, I dressed quickly and headed down to the lobby of my building, where I knew he would be waiting to pick me up.

CHAPTER TWELVE

Katie

I spent the next few months in a whirlwind of romance and blissful happiness. I was in love and couldn't believe just how lucky I was. Ever since I returned from Paris, I had been by Matt's side—in fact, I never wanted to leave that side for a minute. After the crushing blow of Ben's refusal to commit, I hadn't had any expectations going into that dinner with Matt, but that date had been the beginning of a wonderful romance.

Though it had taken a little while for my heart to settle after my roller coaster of a trip to Paris, once I had decided I was all in with Matt, I had fallen hard. It wasn't difficult to see why—he was kind and generous, and most importantly, he adored me. I loved him wholeheartedly, and I couldn't imagine being with anyone else. Every now and then our sex life left a little to be desired, but our emotional connection more than made up for it. He would do anything for me, and that was what I had been looking for my whole life.

It wasn't just the whirlwind romance that had changed my life over the course of the past few months. My celebrity clientele had quadrupled since the pop star attended the awards show in her dress. The pop star herself had put in more orders not just for evening wear, but casual attire as well. Her endorsement of my company had skyrocketed business for me. I could still remember when I saw one of my sundresses in a magazine being worn by a socialite while vacationing in Europe. It had been the best feeling in the world, and I had almost died with excitement when I saw it. I tore the page out of the magazine and framed it—I was a geek like that.

With my company firmly in business and growing every day, I was able to focus more on my relationship with Matt. We had gone to the Hamptons to vacation rather frequently, and I had even been introduced to his parents while there. It hadn't been nerve-wracking at all; I felt completely comfortable and at ease with them, just as I did with Matt.

When I first started to date Matt more seriously, I made the decision not to tell him about Ben. What I had thought was two people falling in love had turned out to be two people just having some kind of fling. While it might have taken my bruised heart a little bit of time to accept it, I knew there was no possibility of a future with Ben. What was the point in telling Matt about some fling I had before we got together? It might upset him unnecessarily, and that was the last thing that I wanted to do.

The one thing I had found shocking about Ben was that I had never heard from him after we parted at the airport. I had thought he would come to his senses and apologize, but he never called. That's what made me finally realize that he had never been the one; he had never really wanted me in the way that I wished. Otherwise, he would have come back for me instead of allowing me to walk out of his life. Months had gone by without so much as a word from him, and it had broken my heart. Though I had my blossoming relationship with Matt to help mend my heart, I hadn't truly realized just how much I had cared for Ben until he was really gone from my life. I had hoped he would come back, but he never did.

So the last thing I wanted to do was hurt a man that actually did care about me. If he knew that I went off to Paris with another man when we were seeing each other, he would be hurt. Even though we hadn't talked about being exclusive at that point, I didn't want to hurt him over my own foolishness. That's exactly what following Ben had been—foolish.

I took a look at myself in the mirror and felt pleased with what I saw. I was wearing a sundress in a shade of blue that complemented my blonde hair. Just then, Matt walked through my bedroom door and whistled. I turned, smiling as he admired me. I had been thinking about asking Matt to move in with me, but after what happened between Ben and me, I was a little gun-shy.

"You look incredible, sweetheart. I must be the luckiest man in the world."

"No, I'm the lucky one, Matt." I walked over to him and kissed him fully on the mouth.

"Then I guess we're both lucky."

We were heading out to dinner together at an Italian restaurant that Matt had picked out. I was looking forward to getting lobster linguine and some wine. Later I would be spending the night at Matt's place.

During dinner, we chatted about an upcoming fashion show I was putting on. It was going to be a big one for me, and there were some serious names that were going to be in attendance. My new spring line was right around the corner, and I needed the show to go off flawlessly. I may end up seeing more than one dress in the magazines this year with the way things were going. I was the newest name in fashion these days, and people were definitely talking about me.

Matt was looking at me adoringly, and I smiled back at him. "I have something to ask you, Katie."

"Of course, what is it?"

"I've thought a lot about this moment. I've been searching for the right time, but I can't keep waiting for the perfect moment."

"What's going on?"

He slid a box across the table, and I recognized it right away as a Tiffany box. I could barely breathe as I stared down at it. My heart started pounding, and I was momentarily speechless.

"Oh my god."

He chuckled. "Are you going to open it?"

I slowly opened the box and gasped. It was a three-karat solitaire diamond on a platinum band. I couldn't believe what I was looking at. There I had been, worried about asking him to move in with me, and he had been planning to ask me to marry him.

"From the moment I met you, Katie, I knew that I wanted to marry you. I know this may seem fast, but I have no doubt in my mind that I want you to be mine forever. Will you marry me?"

I stared at Matt, unable to fully comprehend what he was asking. Was this really happening? I didn't know if it was too soon or not. All I wanted was to be happy, and right at that moment, Matt made me gloriously happy. So why was it that when he asked me, Ben's face flashed through my mind? Why would I think of him instead of reveling in the moment with Matt? I didn't want to even think about why I would think of another man when Matt asked me to marry him.

Fear struck me, but I shook it off, not wanting to think about what it might mean. Instead, I wanted to erase the thought from my mind entirely. This was everything I had ever wanted—I didn't want to ruin it by delving into something that might not mean anything at all.

I had stared at him for so long that he smiled nervously. "You're not going to say no, are you?"

I shook off the thoughts and smiled back at him. "Gosh, I'm sorry. You totally caught me off guard. I would love to be your wife, Matt."

"Oh, thank god."

"I'm so happy." I giggled.

He leaned over and kissed me as tears streamed down my face, and he slipped the ring on my finger.

AFTER SUCH A ROMANTIC and inspiring dinner, we couldn't wait to get back to Matt's studio apartment. As soon as the door shut, we were tearing each other's clothes off. Our mouths found one another with an intensity I hadn't felt in a long time, and it propelled my emotions to a whole other level. His mouth found my breasts, sucking at my hard nipples, and my body arched into his as he did it. I ached between my legs and willed for him to enter me.

"Baby, please, do it now." I didn't care if I was still half-dressed; I needed him right then.

"I love when you talk like that."

I kissed him again, and the feeling of his tongue in my mouth made me instantly wet. His hard body was pressed against mine. He lifted me up into his arms, and my legs circled his waist. He impaled me on his cock, and I moaned loudly.

"Oh Matt, that's so good."

"That's all for you, baby."

"Give it to me, Matt, oh please. That's really good."

He must have had insane upper-body strength to keep me in his arms to fuck me properly. He did an amazing job because I was spent as I wrapped myself around him while he was still inside me.

"I love you, Katie," he whispered.

"I love you too, Matt," I whispered back.

He carried me to the bed and slipped me off him, laying me down before him. I wanted him back inside me badly—I could barely stand to wait. We were engaged now, and I needed him to show me how good our life would be together. His tongue found its way into my mouth once again, and I moaned with desire.

His kisses grew more passionate, and I matched them as best I could. I didn't know if it was the proposal or what, but I felt even more electrified than normal with our lovemaking. His hands were on my body, undressing me properly. He tossed my dress onto the floor and found my nipples with his mouth.

He went back and forth between my breasts before moving slowly down my stomach. He was planning on going down on me, and the thought made me just about crazy. I knew it wasn't his favorite thing to do, and I couldn't wait. Goose bumps prickled my flesh as he kissed my inner thighs. As he got closer to my pussy, he started biting down on my thigh and I loved the feeling. I cried out in what should have been a moan but was almost a growl. He bent down and took my clit into his mouth, nipping gently and then sucking on it. My eyes fluttered closed, and I took a moment to enjoy the sensation.

Matt was a wonderful lover, and he always took care of all my needs. I didn't have to worry about getting an orgasm with him—he made sure I was satisfied with our lovemaking. Waves of pleasure were consuming my whole body, and I was relieved to let my mind shut off and have my body take over. I was on fire like I hadn't been for a long time. I could spend all day in bed with Matt when he was like this. Sex was always exciting and tender—exactly what I needed.

He licked at the lips of my pussy, teasing me slightly. He dipped his tongue inside me, causing me to moan loudly. "God, Matt, that feels so good."

He went back to sucking on my clit while he slipped two fingers inside of my pussy and began pumping fast. He was fucking me so good that I could barely think straight. My breath quickened and I gasped, relishing the feeling of his fingers inside of me.

"Fuck me," I whispered.

He instantly flipped me on my side and put one of my legs on either side of him before he moved closer to me. He entered me from that position, and his cock went in deep. I moaned loudly as his cock stretched inside me. He pumped inside of me fast and hard, and I adored the feeling. I couldn't keep up—the moans were escaping me unchecked. God, the man could drive me wild when he wanted to, and I loved every minute of these moments when he was giving me his all.

He didn't waste any time when he pulled out, and I quickly moved onto my back. I moved over him as he lay down. I wanted him more than ever, and I was going to take what I wanted. My hands went to his chest, and I slid onto his cock slowly. He groaned with enjoyment, and I rode him hard as I moved up and down on his thighs. I smiled down at him sexily, and he looked up at me like I ruled the world. It was intoxicating to be adored, and I loved the feeling. Every time I ground onto his cock, he thrust his hips toward me, meeting each one head on. He was inside of me deep, rubbing against my G-spot, and I could feel an orgasm building inside me. I cried out as the orgasm crashed through me and I soaked Matt's cock.

He sat up slowly, and I knew that he wanted to try another position. I was all for it. I leaned back and braced myself on the bed with my arms behind me. I didn't get off his cock at any point during our position change. He braced himself up with his hands behind his back while I put one leg on either side of him.

The position was intended to create intimacy between two lovers by positioning oneself close enough to kiss the other person. It was one of my favorite positions; I absolutely loved being so close to him in that way. Plus, it gave us both an excellent view of the other, and I could admire Matt's sculpted body—it was something to behold. The man was hot as hell, and I couldn't get enough of looking at his body. I tried as best as I could to keep eye contact with him even as he thrust inside me deep. He felt so good, and I moaned loudly every time he thrust inside me.

I rode his cock, having total control of the speed and intensity of our fucking. It felt so good; I loved the feeling of being in control. It wasn't something I was used to having in the bedroom as this wasn't one of his favorite positions. He moved one hand so that he could play with my clit while I fucked him. I couldn't deny he felt incredible, and knowing this was the man I was going to marry definitely upped the intensity.

I closed my eyes as another orgasm took hold of me. I arched my head back, my hair cascading down my back, and felt him spill into me.

We were both breathing heavily. "That was great," I whispered.

"Yes sweetheart, it was."

I curled up against him and lay my head on his chest. I couldn't help but think that ever since Ben brought me to orgasm for the first time it was as if he had awakened something in me. I'd always be grateful to him for that, at least.

We were still lying in bed later that night when Matt brought in some delicious chocolate ice cream so that we could watch the nightly news together. It had sort of become a habit of ours before we retired for the night. To my surprise, while watching the news, I saw Ben on TV and my breath caught. I focused on what they were saying and realized that the news was discussing Ben's court case and upcoming trial. In fact, they were discussing the fact that there would not be an upcoming trial because Ben had been acquitted of the charges and the case was being dropped.

I couldn't believe what I was hearing. I felt pure joy about the whole thing and knew that it would take a lot of stress off Ben's shoulders. I was really happy for him. I felt like jumping for joy at the news but held back because Matt had no idea that I even knew Ben at all. Well, at least now Ben could go back to the company and do what he wanted with it without having the charges hanging over his head.

Matt spoke up, to my surprise. "This guy is a real piece of work. The shit he gets away with is unreal. I wonder how much money it took to get him out of those charges."

I couldn't believe what I was hearing. I hadn't realized Matt even knew of Ben or the charges against him. I didn't like what I was hearing at all though. "What are you talking about?"

"This billionaire—he goes out and poisons the ocean, and somehow he manages to get off scot-free. Amazing. Obviously he knew what was going on—it was his company. I thought for sure they would throw the book at him, but money will buy you out of anything."

I cleared my throat. "Matt, you don't know that. You don't know him at all—how can you be so harsh when you don't know what really happened?"

He narrowed his eyes at me, confusion clouding them. "Why do you care what I think, sweetheart? It's not the first time I've called someone out on the news. What's so different about this guy?"

I felt suddenly guilty all over again. I shouldn't have said anything because he was right. It wasn't the first time he had talked about someone on the news, and now I just looked defensive. I shouldn't even be arguing the issue—I no longer had ties to Ben, and he had dropped me without another thought, so why was I defending the guy? I had originally planned on letting go of Matt for Ben, and look how well that turned out. I probably would have lost everything had I made that choice.

"Katie? Is everything okay?"

"Sorry. I actually know Ben. That's why I spoke up."

"You're kidding me. How?"

"Remember how I told you that I went on that AIDS mission a while back?"

He nodded.

"Well, Ben was there. He was volunteering his time as well. That's where I met him."

"Right. I actually heard about that. He did it just to save face after the scandal broke out. It's funny I never put two and two together before."

"Well, there's actually more to the story. I never told you this because I didn't think it mattered at the time, but while we were there, we sort of had a fling. It lasted a while after as well. I ended things with him, before you and I got serious together."

He looked at me, shocked. "What are you talking about? I can't imagine you would be involved with someone like him."

"Matt, don't be like that. I'm sorry I didn't tell you, I just didn't think it was a big deal. You and I had just met, and I was still involved with him. I just didn't want to hurt you by telling you about the whole thing. It was really nothing."

"And yet you're telling me about this now. Why?"

"Well, because of the look on your face mainly. I felt guilty about getting defensive, and, well, I guess I should have told you from the get-go. I would rather we be upfront about everything before we get married, so there are no secrets."

It was obvious he was pissed at me, and he was probably right to be so. I just didn't want it to affect our relationship. I had just wanted to be honest with him, but maybe that had been a mistake.

"Katie, I can hardly imagine you with a man like that. I

almost wish you hadn't told me." He looked so confused that it broke my heart. He was just so good—maybe I didn't deserve him after all.

"I'm sorry. I didn't want to hurt you." I leaned over and kissed him on the lips. I looked into his eyes and said, "I would never do anything to hurt you. So forgive me, please—just don't be mad at me."

He sighed. "Katie, I love you, and I'm going to marry you. Of course I forgive you. I just didn't expect anything like this."

"I know, I'm sorry. You need to know that I only want you." I nuzzled into his neck and could smell his cologne. I leaned back up and kissed him again. Matt shut off the TV, and we lay back down together. I knew it wasn't as simple as that—I had hurt him after all, but at least I had been honest about the whole thing. We didn't need those kinds of secrets between us. I worried that he would lie awake that night thinking about Ben and I, and I didn't want that. There was nothing I could do about it though. It would be up to me to make him forget all that—I would just love him as much as possible. I sighed deeply and nuzzled closer to Matt as I started to fall asleep.

CHAPTER THIRTEEN

Katie

F*our months later*

I WAS AT AN AIDS FUNDRAISER, and the room was jam-packed with people all around. I was weeks away from my wedding, and it was the only thing that occupied my mind. I was trying to focus on the event, but all I was thinking about was the dress I had designed for my wedding. It was almost ready, and I was excited to see myself in it.

"My god, your ass looks great in that dress, Katie."

Shocked, I turned to see the man behind the comment, and my mouth dropped to the floor. Ben was there, standing right behind me, and seeing him caused my breath to catch. It pissed me off that he was still as handsome as the last time I'd seen him. Why did he have such a hold on me still? Just seeing him there made my heart beat out of my chest.

"Is that any way to talk to a lady?"

"I just wanted to catch your attention, that's all."

Ben had always been that dreamy guy that you couldn't get enough of, and that didn't seem to change no matter how long we stayed away from each other. He had an easy smile that always made me feel safe, even though it was the last feeling I should have around him. I suddenly wished that I had insisted that Matt come to the event, even though he had to work. I hadn't expected Ben to be there, otherwise I would have.

"What are you doing here, Ben?"

"Aside from letting you know you have a great ass? I would think that would be obvious?"

I rolled my eyes. "I hope you aren't here for me. I'm an engaged woman now, soon to be married. The wedding is in a few weeks."

His eyes narrowed at me. "Yes, I had heard something like that through the grapevine. You don't think you might be rushing into things? You couldn't have been dating more than a few months—unless you were with him while we were together."

"I wasn't. Not that I have to explain any of that to you."

"You don't need to be so hostile toward me, Katie. I'm not here to hurt you." Ben moved in closer to me, and suddenly my heart started to beat faster than I was comfortable with. He was currently invading my space, and it made me feel a little unsteady.

"I don't mean to be hostile, but we didn't leave each other on the best of terms."

"My fault, I know. I was a little upset at your departure."

I nodded, unsure of what else there was to say.

"Do you want to go somewhere and talk? I promise you won't regret it."

He was whispering in my ear, and chills ran up my spine. How did he still have such an effect on me after all this time? It puzzled me to no end. I pushed him away from me, and I was finally able catch my breath.

"No, thanks. I think I would like to stay with the party."

He chuckled and I couldn't help but enjoy the twinkle he had in his eyes when he focused them on me. Ben moved toward me, and I took a step back, feeling confused. He was still smiling, as if he was a predator seeking out his prey.

"You're not curious as to what I might have to say?"

"No. I can't imagine what you could say to me at this point. What's done is done."

"Have a drink with me. C'mon, we're both in a room full of strangers."

"I don't think that's a very good idea."

Ben moved in close to me again, and I wondered if I was going to be okay. He had a problem with personal space, and it was affecting me greatly. Chills went up my spine as his hand grazed my cheek. My skin tingled when he lifted his hand away. My throat felt dry, and I was rendered completely speechless.

"I think you get more beautiful every time I see you, Katie."

I was having a hard time thinking. I wasn't sure what had come over me, but I knew that being around Ben in any manner was a bad idea. I couldn't allow myself to get sucked in by him. I had always loved the way he talked to me, but those days were over and I needed to move on with my life. I was getting married, for goodness' sake—I shouldn't even be having a conversation with Ben. What would Matt think?

Ben must have had a ton of eligible women around him all the time. Women who would die to be on his arm even if it was for just one night—so why did he keep coming back for me? It was maddening having a man pursue me when I had no idea what he wanted from me. We were on totally different pages all the time, and yet he kept coming back into my life. It had to end.

I felt his hand move to the small of my back, and I gasped when warmth followed after.

"We could be so hot together, Katie, if you just let it happen." He was whispering in my ear again, and his hand moved to my ass when he did so, squeezing it gently. I gasped.

I pushed him off me, feeling my blood boil in the process. When I did, I knocked into his arm and the drink he was carrying tipped. My mouth dropped as the drink spilled down the front of me.

"Oh shit," muttered Ben.

I looked down at my dress in horror and felt like crying.

"You idiot. How could you?"

Ben quickly turned to find some napkins on a nearby table. When he returned, he started dabbing at my breasts. I snatched the napkin out of his hand and glared at him. I was absolutely furious with him. My night was going downhill fast.

"What on earth do you think you're doing? Look at my dress, Ben—and you want to cop a feel now?"

He chuckled and it made me want to strangle him. "Calm down. I wasn't trying to feel you up. I feel terrible about the drink, and I was only trying to help."

"Oh, well, thank god you were here. I'm going to have to go home now before the party has even started. Just look what you did to it. You are driving me insane!"

"That could be a good thing, right?"

"Ugh! Just leave me be, Ben."

He grabbed my arm, and it took my attention away from the dress. "Katie, I'm sorry. I didn't mean to spill the drink on you. I would never want to ruin your night."

"Well, did you think it was appropriate to grab my ass? I'm not a single woman any longer."

"I thought you might like it. You used to like it. I just can't imagine you marrying that guy."

I couldn't help but shake my head. He really was trying to make me lose my mind that much was obvious. I had never seen anyone more confident than Ben, and for some stupid reason it was still so appealing to me. There was some weird gravitational pull between us, and I couldn't deny it even if I wanted to. It didn't help that he was an exceptionally good-looking man. But the moment he opened his mouth, I felt like slapping him. I had no idea how it felt to walk around so self-assured all the time, but Ben had it down to a tee. He wasn't fazed at all by the fact that I was so unimpressed with him.

"Aren't you going to congratulate me on my acquittal?"

I softened a bit when he said that. "I actually saw that on the news. Congratulations. I was very happy to see that you were going to be okay."

"Thank you."

Ben brushed my hair behind my ear, and I looked up at him with surprise. His touch was like having electricity move through my body. I never felt that way with Matt. With him, it was always about feeling safe—and that was the way you wanted to feel with your spouse, right?

I looked up into his eyes, and my breathing became labored. My heart started beating fast in my chest, and my dress was all but forgotten. I needed him to back off, to give me some space. I was overwhelmed by Ben, especially having him so close to me.

"Look, you need to stop touching me. What's wrong with you? You can't just put your hands on me whenever you want."

He smiled and the way he was looking at me stopped me from speaking. "I always loved how sassy you were. I miss that."

"Oh please, Ben, spare me."

"I do."

I threw my hands up in the air, feeling beyond frustrated with him.

He laughed. "Look, I can help you with the dress. There is no reason you have to leave. C'mon, I have an idea. We'll fix that dress if I have to suck every last drop out of it."

I couldn't believe the things that came out of his mouth. I couldn't help but laugh. Ben grabbed my hand and led me through groups of people. I blushed furiously at the thought that people were seeing me so unhinged—and with a cocktail down the front of me no less. I knew I needed to get away from Ben as quickly as possible. He was trouble, and I shouldn't be going anywhere with him. How had I managed to get tangled up with him again in a matter of minutes? He always seemed to have such a power over me that I just followed him wherever he went.

We slipped into the hallway, and Ben still held my hand as if he was saving me from something. It wasn't long before we found the women's bathroom, and we slipped inside.

"I really don't think I need you in here, Ben. What if someone walks in?"

I pulled my hand from his and instantly felt the absence of it. It made me feel sad that there was a level of longing there still. I sighed deeply and watched him as he turned on the tap and tested the temperature. He then grabbed some paper towels and dampened them enough they wouldn't make my dress any worse than it was—which was saying a lot. The stain wasn't that horrible—at least he hadn't been drinking Coke.

I watched as he dabbed lightly on my dress, and I almost smiled as he did so. No—I was not going to let myself get pulled in by him again. The stain was actually disappearing, but now my dress was wet, which wasn't much better. It looked terrible, and I felt tears spring up in my eyes.

"The stain is gone, thank you."

"I told you it would work out."

"It's wet, Ben. I can't go out like this."

He took a look around the bathroom and smiled. I looked to where he was looking and couldn't help but smile with him. "This will work," he said.

"You're brilliant."

"I know," he said with a wink. He pulled me over to the dryer and pushed the button. Hot air blasted onto the dress, and I watched as it started to dry. I had to give him some credit for the quick thinking. I couldn't be happier that the issue was being solved. I had just arrived at the party and didn't want to return home so early. I was hoping to enjoy myself and do some good for a great cause. I was determined to enjoy myself whether Ben was there to annoy me or not.

"It's working, thank god. You're lucky, because I was going to kill you."

"Right, that wouldn't have been good. You're welcome though. I'm glad I could help. I hope the dress isn't ruined."

I was about to answer him when I felt his warmth behind me. He was so close that I could feel his breath against my neck. His mouth was close to my ear when he whispered, "There's just something about you, Katie. I go nuts when I'm around you. Being near you feels right—I know you can feel it too."

My eyes fluttered closed, and the heat from his body so close to mine ignited a fire inside of me. I felt dizzy, and when his hands found their way to my ass, I thought I might faint.

"So firm."

I gasped. I did not want to be feeling this way with him, but my body felt completely different. I wanted to be consumed by him in every way. One minute I had been appalled by what he did to my dress, and the next I was okay with his hands on my body.

I shuddered beneath his touch and allowed myself to feel everything my body was telling me. I was burning up, and I could barely stand it. There was a throb between my legs that I hadn't felt in some time. Things were just different between Matt and me—not bad, just not all-consuming. That was a good thing though—I didn't need to feel like I was in another world all the time. Matt was someone that would keep me safe no matter what. And what's more, Matt actually wanted me—all the time, not just when it was convenient.

I tried to shake off the sensations coursing through my body and listen to my head. I needed to stop things before they got out of control. I did not want to be feeling anything for Ben. He was the one who had walked away from me without a word. It had been his choice. He couldn't just keep coming back into my life and confusing me like that. I had always been so attracted to him though, but where had that ever gotten me? I just continued to get hurt by him. I turned around suddenly, forcing his hands to leave my ass. He pushed me against the wall.

"Ben, stop, we can't do this."

It was like he didn't hear me as he smiled and bent down to kiss me. His kiss was just how I remembered it to be—warm and inviting. I kissed him back and felt the same passion and intensity between us. I had never felt so raw in all my life—he just opened me up again. We kept kissing and those kisses were taking my breath away. I pushed against his chest, knowing that I had to put a stop to it.

"Sweetheart, what's wrong? You feel so incredible."

"It's too much, Ben. I can't do this, and you know that."

"That's not true. You want this—I know you do. You are with the wrong man. How can you not see that?"

He smiled as he bent down to me again. I had zero control at that moment, and I was losing the ability to care. I wanted to be consumed, and he was confusing me. Why was he so confident that I belonged with him when he had yet to claim me? Would it be so bad to just let go with him, let him claim me? I could barely think straight anymore, and when he kissed me, I had to wonder if I had made the wrong choice. If Matt was the one, then how could I feel this intensity with another man? I couldn't remember the last time I had felt that way before, but it was a feeling I only ever thought about when Ben was around. I longed for the passion that I felt with Ben, but he was a loose cannon, someone I couldn't depend on.

Ben continued to kiss me, tasting my lips over and over again. I could smell his musky scent, and it drove me crazy. He cupped my chin and kissed my mouth gently. We started off softly but then continued with increasing intensity. His mouth pressed hard against mine, and I moaned softly. His hands were in my hair, tugging gently. We were so close together, it was like we were one. Ben's tongue entered my mouth and played with mine. He took my tongue into his mouth, and he sucked on it slowly. I moaned, eager to have him. His kisses consumed me as he licked and nipped at my lips. I was losing control—I could feel it. I felt paralyzed beneath his touch, and I wasn't sure how much more I could take. He had total control of my body, and I didn't think that I could pull away even if I wanted to. I just knew that I needed him more than anything. He was such a good kisser; I had almost forgotten.

Ben cupped my breasts in his hands and kneaded them. My nipples grew hard underneath his touch.

"You make me insane, Katie. Your body is incredible. I want you out of that dress."

I gasped in shock. Did he really think we were going to have sex in the bathroom? I glanced toward the door, surprised we hadn't already been discovered. I wasn't sure what I would do if someone walked in on us right then. I would be so embarrassed.

The thoughts that ran through my mind were also embarrassing. I wanted him, and the images going through my brain were taking over any rational thought I might have. I couldn't believe that Ben had managed to get me pinned up against a wall in the women's bathroom. I knew that I should get away from him, pull away and run out of the bathroom. That would be the best thing I could do, but I couldn't bring myself to do it. My physical side had completely taken over, and I wanted to be there with him. I enjoyed his hands on my body, and I had to admit to myself that I had missed him terribly. His tongue explored my mouth, and I felt lost inside.

He began to lift my dress, and I froze. He was going to try to have sex with me right then and there. Would I let him?

His hands were on my ass once again, and I moaned against his kisses. I heard voices outside of the door, and that snapped me immediately back to reality.

"Wait, stop. There's someone outside."

He froze and it sounded like someone was about to come into the bathroom. I looked down at myself and was so angry with myself that I had allowed myself to be in that position. I pushed him off me and fled the bathroom, almost running into a woman coming in. Ben called out after me, but I kept going until I found myself outside of the hotel and looking for a cab.

CHAPTER FOURTEEN

Katie

I woke up and lay there in bed, realizing that I was going to be getting married the next morning. My god, it had come quick, sneaking up on me when I had least expected it. One minute I had been single, and the next I was there, a day away from getting married. I couldn't believe how time had flown, though we hadn't had a long engagement at all. In fact, it had been only a few months—it was just what we had wanted. I had wondered though if maybe a longer engagement would have been better so I had a clearer picture of my future.

What had happened between Ben and me at the AIDS benefit had confused me more than ever. I had stayed up all night tossing and turning. I couldn't figure out what had happened between us or why I was so connected to Ben. I didn't have that feeling with Matt, and that was what kept me up at night. I worried that maybe there was something wrong with our relationship. I knew that I loved Matt, but did I love someone else more? We just didn't have the same kind of intense physical and mental connection as I did with Ben. Was that a bad thing? Or was it just something that lots of people learned to live without? I wasn't sure. It had bothered me for days until I got back into the groove of my daily routine and just chose not to think about it any longer.

I crawled out of bed and started to get ready. I dressed quickly, knowing that I had to get going. I had a lot to accomplish that day to get myself ready to be married the next day. I had all kinds of nervous butterflies in my stomach, and it made me a little uneasy.

I hadn't heard from Ben again after the AIDS benefit. That was typical though. It continued to baffle me more and more how he was able to just come and go. I had no idea what he wanted from me. If it wasn't love, then what continued to pull him to me all the time? In Paris, he just wanted things to be casual, which was something he could have with anyone, so why did he keep coming back to me? It wasn't fair to me. I felt lost with him, and the fact that he continued to leave without answering left me confused. Technically I was the one that had walked out on him the last time in the bathroom, but it wouldn't have been hard for him to come and find me and explain himself. But just like after Paris, I never heard back from him.

So what did it all mean? Had he been coming back for me once and for all, or was he still hoping for a casual arrangement with me? It was something that plagued my mind. I would have loved to have had some closure from him before I married Matt, but sometimes you just never got what you wanted in life. I would be marrying the man I loved tomorrow whether I got closure or not. I just wished I had some idea about what was going through his mind and why he sought me out. He had told me that I was with the wrong guy, which implied that he wanted me to be with him. But did he really, or was I just some prize that he was trying to win? Ben could be very territorial at times, and knowing that I was marrying another man could be all it took for him to start sniffing around me again.

I had no evidence that Ben felt anything but lust for me, and that was why I chose to go ahead with my wedding despite what happened at the AIDS benefit. I would need to tell Ben at some point that he could not come around any longer. He was just causing trouble, and I didn't want anything to get in the way of my future marriage or happiness with Matt. Whether I liked it or not, I would need to remove Ben from my life forever.

After a long day of rushing around like a chicken with my head cut off, I was back at my apartment trying to wind down from all the excitement. All the last-minute details were organized, and now all I wanted to do was relax. I was thoroughly exhausted. I probably should have had the bridesmaids handle the last-minute arrangements, but I was a bit of a perfectionist when it came to these things, so I handled it all on my own. All I wanted now was a peaceful night at home with a bottle of wine. Tomorrow I would be marrying the man I loved and starting our future together.

I had to say no to my bridal party's idea of taking me out for the night. I wasn't into all of the bachelorette party hooplas. I didn't want to be out all night, nor did I want to wake up on my wedding day tired and hungover—it just wasn't worth it to me. They had offered to just take me out for dinner, but I wasn't in the mood for it. I just wanted to spend some time with myself and reflect on the future. Having a couple of glasses of wine would be the perfect relaxation to get me ready for my big day.

I wouldn't have much more time in the apartment anyway—in a few weeks I would officially be moving in with Matt. I would miss my place after having been there for many years, but once the honeymoon was over, I would be living with my husband. I just wanted to enjoy some time alone in my apartment before I had to say goodbye to all the memories I had accumulated there.

I opened the bottle and poured some wine into a glass. Taking a sip from it, I wondered if we had rushed into getting married. Matt had wanted to do it right away, even suggesting to me that we elope immediately. I wasn't into the idea—it is my first wedding and all, I wanted to have all my friends and family in attendance. I knew my father would have been quite upset had I gone off and eloped. The only thing I could suggest to Matt was that we plan a wedding that could happen right away. We were only engaged for a few months before I started to plan a wedding that would happen in another month's time. Now that I was thinking about it, I wondered why Matt had been so anxious to tie the knot. Had he been afraid of losing me even back then? I couldn't imagine it. He hadn't even known about Ben at that point.

So, in the end, I had agreed to a quickie wedding and hired a wedding planner to get the job done. We sent out the wedding invitations immediately, and they started coming back just as quickly. My parents had accepted Matt immediately because they saw the things in him that I had seen when I met him. They believed in his character and thought I had made a wonderful choice in a partner. At the time it hadn't seemed rushed, but now I wasn't so sure that it had been the best course of action. It wasn't that I didn't love Matt—because I did, wholeheartedly—but my recent encounter with Ben had made me question a lot of things. Why did I still react to him that way? That was what worried me the most. I didn't like the fact that another man could make me react with such intensity that I was powerless in his arms. That should be the kind of reaction I got from my husband, shouldn't it?

I sat on my couch sipping wine and thinking about the wonderful future that Matt and I could have. I just needed to focus on that, and everything would work out just the way it was supposed to. The wedding would be flawless, and I had very little I needed to worry about on the day because it was all in the hands of the wedding planner. After the wedding, we would be flying off to Spain for our honeymoon. I had never been to Spain before, and I couldn't be more excited about our little adventure there. It was so exciting that I could barely stand to wait. It would be a great start to us creating our own memories for our future. I was making the right decision, I just knew it.

I looked up in surprise when there was a knock on the door. I had no idea who would show up the night before my wedding, unannounced. I had made it clear to Matt that he was not to come and see me before the wedding, so I knew that it wasn't him. Puzzled, I got up from the couch and headed for the door. I swung it open and wished that I had ignored it altogether. My mouth hit the floor, and I couldn't believe my luck.

"You have to be kidding me. What the hell are you doing here?"

Ben stood at the door, looking rather sheepish for a change. Not that it mattered—just the sight of him angered me in more ways than one. I debated slamming the door in his face but decided against it. What was he thinking coming here? What if Matt had been here? I wondered if he knew it was the night before my wedding, because his timing was truly epic.

"Can we talk?"

"Ugh! Why the hell not, right, Ben? You must be kidding me here. I can't believe the absolute nerve of you." I stomped back into my apartment, leaving him standing at the door. I plopped down on the couch and drank half of the glass of wine that I had poured earlier.

He stepped inside and I realized I was shaking all over. I couldn't remember a time when I was angrier. The fact that he had shown up at my place like that drove me insane. The thing that made me the angriest, however, was the fact that I realized as soon as I saw him on the other side of the door that I was in love with him. He continued to stand there, not saying a thing, and it was starting to nag at me.

"I suggest you start talking before I kick you out."

He sighed deeply, looking sadder than ever. I had never seen him in such a state. Usually he was overly confident around me.

"I love you, Katie. I always have. I've just been so stupid."

For a moment, I thought I might throw up. I couldn't believe what was happening right before my eyes on the eve of my wedding day. It was preposterous.

"Don't you dare say that to me now. How could you?"

"I'm sorry, baby. I really am. I'm a mess and this is all my fault. But it's true—I think I've loved you since the moment I met you."

"Oh my god. Do you realize this is the night before my wedding day? How could you be so selfish? Why are you doing this to me?"

"I'm not trying to hurt you. I'm just trying not to lose the best thing that has ever happened to me. I've been fighting my feelings for so long as I tried to navigate my life and the company. I'm an idiot and I know that. I almost lost my mind when I saw your wedding announcement. You can't marry this guy, Katie."

Tears sprang up in my eyes. "Stop this."

"I know I'm a complete shit for doing this, but don't go through with something that's a mistake. You don't have to. Be with me. I will take care of you. I tried to let you go, but I can't do it any longer. I need you, Katie."

My heart was beating out of my chest, and I was so angry that I thought I would tear the room apart. How could he do this to me? I had tried to be with him so many times, and he had failed me over and over again. How could he ask this of me now?

I screamed at him, my face burning. "Why couldn't you have come back months ago? Why didn't you come to me after the AIDS benefit? Honestly, Ben, what the hell is wrong with you?"

He shrugged, at a loss for words himself. "Don't marry him," he whispered.

"Why not? He loves me and I love him too. He wanted to take care of me when you were too busy being 'casual' with me. You didn't want the whole package with me—you just wanted fun. Now that I'm about to be married, you want to come back? Why? So that you can leave again when you grow bored?"

"I could never grow bored of you. We have a real connection, Katie—you know that."

"And yet it wasn't strong enough for you to stay with me."

"You can't marry him. It wouldn't be fair to him. You can't deny that you love me too, maybe more than him. How could you marry another man when you have such strong feelings for me?"

"You don't know the first thing about being fair, Ben." I was shaking my head, completely disgusted with him. We stood there in front of each another, just staring the other down. Ben stood there calmly while my heart was thrashing around in my rib cage. I tried to control my emotions, but it wasn't easy. He was right, I did love him, but he was not a stable partner at all. I would always worry that he would leave me, and I didn't need that kind of person in my life.

Tears streamed down my face. "How could you do this, Ben?"

He shook his head slowly. "I have no explanation, no good one anyway. I'm sorry I fucked up. There's nothing else I can say. But it will never happen again, I promise you. I should never have let you walk out of my life in Paris—it was the worst mistake of my life. I thought I had the time to figure things out, you know? I would never have thought you would be engaged a few months after Paris. Has it not occurred to you that you may have rushed into it? Maybe that's my fault as well."

I felt angry all over again. I was furious that he was questioning my decision even though I had wondered about it myself. I just didn't want him to have the satisfaction of knowing that.

"I don't think we're rushing things at all. Matt is a great guy. He knows how to treat a woman properly."

"No, he rushed this in order to trap you. There's no other reason why he would get married within a few months of meeting you. He just doesn't want you to change your mind, and you will. I guarantee it. You guys don't have what we do."

"How do you know?"

"I know. I know because of how you kiss me."

"Stop it. He's not trapping me."

"You guys have only been engaged a few months. How well do you even know him?"

"That doesn't matter. We fell in love, and that won't change."

He narrowed his gaze at me, and I knew that I had hurt him. I could tell he wanted to say more but was worried he might go too far and push me away. I knew that the thought of me being in love with someone else probably made him crazy. I wasn't sure how I would feel if I found out that Ben was marrying someone else, but I doubted that I would feel warm and fuzzy about it.

"Tell me that you don't love me," he said.

"I need you to leave. This is too much for me. It doesn't matter how I feel about you. I told another man that I would marry him, and I won't go back on that promise. Not for someone who has left me so many times."

"Choose me instead—marry me instead, Katie. I love you and I need you to change your mind."

I swallowed hard as I stared at him. My mind was doing flip-flops, and my heart was trying to rip itself out of my chest and reach for him. I wanted him, I knew that much, but I also knew I couldn't trust him, and that was a pretty big deal to me. There was a large part of me that wanted to run off with him, but I couldn't allow myself to be that foolish. I didn't want to give up everything only to have him change his mind on me again. I would not survive being left again—I needed to protect my heart.

"Ben, I chose you already, a few times actually. I was going to tell Matt that things were over between us after Paris, and look what you pulled. Then again at the AIDS benefit, I never heard from you again after that. You said you weren't ready for me, and I don't know that you ever will be. Matt wants me now."

"So you're going to marry another man when you are in love with me?" he yelled, causing me to flinch.

"I love him."

"So how are you going to love him with all your heart when part of it is with me?"

Tears filled my eyes again. "That will go away eventually."

"I doubt that very much. I can feel the chemistry right now between us—you can't deny it, Katie."

"I don't care. It's too late. You waited too long."

"Please, Katie, don't do this."

"We could have been something great, Ben, and I did try to be with you. But I won't hurt Matt when I can't trust you to stay."

"You belong with me."

My mind began to fog up again, and my heart was in so much pain over him. I was torn, but I knew I couldn't allow my heart to make my decisions any longer. I had tried that already, and it didn't work. I needed to get him out of my apartment—I couldn't have this conversation any longer. If Matt decided to come and surprise me anyway, everything would go up in a cloud of smoke once he saw Ben there. I couldn't risk it. Maybe that's what Ben was hoping for all along.

"I need you to go now, Ben. I can't do this anymore."

"Katie, please." He was begging now, and it broke my heart.

I took a deep breath, willing myself to stay strong. "I'm marrying Matt tomorrow. I've made my decision, and you need to respect that. It's time for you to go."

Ben turned from me without another word and walked out the door. He didn't slam it, but instead, he closed it silently. I went to the door and locked it behind him. I pressed my forehead against the cool wood and prayed that I was making the right decision.

"Goodbye, Ben," I whispered.

CHAPTER FIFTEEN

Katie

Ben and I returned from a walk in the park with smiles on our faces. The day had been bright and magical, and I couldn't remember the last time I had felt so happy. There was just something about being around him that completed me in a way that nothing else could.

As soon as we walked into the apartment, Ben whisked me into his arms and kissed me deeply. All I could think about throughout my day was how badly I wanted to be in Ben's arms, and it always came true. We were going to be married shortly, and I couldn't wait to be Mrs. Ben Donovan. It would be the best day of my life, and it couldn't come fast enough. Being his wife felt like something I had been dreaming about for so long, and it was about to come true.

We kissed from the time we left his car all the way up the stairs and into my apartment. I had fumbled with the lock on my door as he kissed my neck. All I wanted to do was tear off all his clothes every time he kissed me. He was driving me half-mad with his mouth, and a simple act of unlocking a door became almost impossible.

Once the door was unlocked, we pushed our way through, and I turned to him, grabbing his face in my hands and kissing his lips passionately. I bit his lower lip, causing him to growl my name.

"Katie, I am going to fuck you so good you are going to pass out."

I moaned and then stopped to stare at him. "I love when you say my name."

"Yes, baby. It's beautiful and I like how it sounds coming out of my mouth as well."

He picked me up in his arms and carried me to the bedroom. He laid me out on the bed and climbed on top of me. His mouth connected with mine once again and brought a searing heat with it.

Suddenly I pulled away and looked him in the eyes, my brow furrowed. "Why do you like me?"

"Katie, are you joking? Are we going to do this right now? You know I absolutely adore you for a million reasons."

"If you want in my pants, you bet your ass we are doing it right now."

He smiled down at me, and I almost forgot the whole thing. "It's because you're so much more than just tits and a pussy."

"Oh, gee, thanks."

He laughed. "No, really. You have a brain and you use it. You're clearly passionate about your career, and you're good at it, might I add. You're dedicated and hardworking. You're different from a lot of girls out there these days who just want a man to take them shopping all the time. You're actually pretty amazing."

"Great answer."

"You know I love you."

"Yes, and I love you too."

His mouth found mine again, and our tongues intermingled. I sucked on his slowly, getting more turned on by the minute. He started undressing and I did the same, watching him lose each article of clothing. God, he was beautiful, and I could finally admire him fully.

I lay there before him, naked, and I was already wet between my legs as I anticipated claiming his cock as my own.

He climbed back on top of me and kissed me hard on the mouth. He began trailing kisses down my jaw line and slowly down my neck. The sensation of his lips against my skin was exhilarating. The softer the kiss, the more goose bumps appeared on my skin. As he kissed his way down to my breasts, his hand went between my legs and he rubbed his fingers against my clit. Pleasure coursed through me, and I moaned.

"Oh baby, you're already wet. God, that's incredible."

I smiled up at him. "Ben, I want you so badly. My body wants you—it knows what's coming."

"Be patient, baby. I want to take my time with you." His mouth found my nipples and sucked on them. He sucked, nipped, and flicked my nipples with his tongue, and I arched my back in ecstasy.

"Please, Ben, fuck me. Put your cock inside me right now."

"Oh, I love when you beg like that. But I'm not ready."

He continued to trail kisses down my stomach and around my navel. Goose bumps popped up all over my skin. He made his way all the way down to my pussy. He spread my legs wide and admired my pussy, open and waiting for him. He looked like he wanted to gobble me up right then and there.

"You look so good. And I know you taste even better." He bent down then and licked me from one end to the other. I moaned loudly. He sucked on my clit and nipped it gently. He stuck two fingers into my pussy and started pumping. I cried out, feeling the buildup of an orgasm. He was incredible and I couldn't get enough of him. I didn't think I could ever get enough of Ben, and he was about to make me cum with just his fingers and mouth.

"Baby, please put your cock in me. I need it."

"Not until you cum in my mouth."

That's all it took for my orgasm to unleash and give him exactly what he asked for. I had never had someone talk to me so dirty before, but I loved the eroticism of it. It added to the already scorching chemistry the two of us shared. There was just something about Ben that drove me crazy—I wanted to be pleased by him in every way possible. He felt incredible inside of me.

"Fuck me now, Ben, fuck me." He pushed his cock deep inside of me, stretching my pussy. "Oh god, you feel good. Your cock... it's so big and so hard, baby. I love it."

He groaned at my words, and I knew I was driving him crazy. He pushed in deeper and pumped me slowly before he picked up the pace a little. He was huge and I ached even more now that he was inside of me. He touched every nerve inside of me, and I moaned loudly as he picked up the pace. I wrapped my legs around him and lifted my hips to meet each thrust of his hard cock.

"Your pussy is so wet, Katie. You feel incredible."

"God, Ben, I'm going to cum again."

He pumped faster, burying his cock inside of me as an intense orgasm rocked me to the core. I cried out his name as waves of pleasure came over me.

I was gasping as he slid out of me. I hated him being gone.

"I think it's my turn to fuck you, Ben."

"Ohh sweetheart, I like the sound of that."

He lay out onto the bed, and it was my turn to climb on top of him. Before I impaled myself on his cock, I bent down and took him in my mouth. I could taste my juices on his cock, and it turned me on even more. I sucked on him hard as I swirled my tongue along his shaft.

"Katie, I love the way you suck my cock. You're so good at it, baby." He was groaning underneath me, and it was making me crazy.

He pulled me up and off his cock. I put myself in position to ride his cock and then sat down on it. He went in deep, and I gasped with him inside me. I began riding him slowly at first, taking my time. I *would slowly slide off until he was almost out of me, and then I went down fast. He groaned with every thrust I made, and then I picked up the pace. I rode his cock hard until I was sure he was going to cum, then slowed down the pace. I wasn't ready for him to cum yet—I still wanted to have more fun. I continued to fuck him slowly, looking down into his eyes. I always found it rare for a man to make eye contact with his lover—sex was so intimate that at times it could be overwhelming for men. That was my experience anyway.*

But Ben was different, and I loved that about him. We were different together, a better couple than most. He looked me dead in the eyes, and the heat that I saw in them drove me crazy. But it wasn't just heat that I saw there, just like what we were doing was no longer just sex. Something had changed between us a long time ago, and it would never be the same again. Whether or not we were ready for the change would be something that we would discover together at a later date. For the time being, we would enjoy what we had and see where it led us. Not that I didn't already know—I would marry that man, and sooner rather than later.

I went back and forth between a slow drawn-out fuck and then riding his cock hard. I could tell by the look on his face that I was driving him crazy, but I loved every moment of pleasing him and I was going to draw it out as much as I could.

"My turn, baby."

I smiled down at him and nodded. I lifted myself off his cock and regretted it immediately. I needed him inside of me at all times. I craved his cock like an addict craved drugs. I wanted to have him inside me now, not in a few seconds, but now.

He moved me into position so that I was lying partially on my side, resting on my forearm and hip. He got off the bed and stood up behind me, like a variation of a doggy-style position. I loved doggy-style; not only was it a deep fuck, but I also liked when Ben had control of fucking me. It made me feel powerless to his every whim, which turned me on intensely.

He pushed his cock inside of me, and I gasped with pleasure.

"Oh yes, baby, that feels so good." I moaned with every thrust he gave me. He was deep and felt fantastic. He started off slow—agonizingly slow—but then he pushed in harder and faster. He pounded into my pussy, causing me to cry out in pleasure. It felt so good, and I wanted him to fuck me like that all night.

"Oh god, Ben, I'm going to cum again."

"Yes, baby, cum all over my cock, darling. I want to feel you. Don't hold back."

I exploded onto his cock as he continued to pound my pussy. As soon as one wave of orgasm passed, another followed suit. Multiple orgasms? This was truly my lucky day.

He fucked me really good, and I could not have asked for a better sexual partner. It was like he had my body mapped out and knew exactly what to do to get me to lose my mind.

"Ben, cum with me."

"You want me to cum, baby?"

"God yes, I want you to pump me full of cum, baby. Please give it to me."

He groaned as he fucked me hard, pushing his cock into me deeper and deeper. He cried out as his own orgasm rocked him into me. He spilled into me, and his rocking slowed down as he brought himself down from the orgasm.

"God, that was good," I whispered.

"I would definitely have to agree with you on that one."

He pulled out of me, and I collapsed on the bed. He followed suit and lay down on the bed beside me. I curled up into his chest and kissed it. He had the musky scent of a man who had sweated, doing a good job of fucking his woman.

"Mmmmm, I liked that," I murmured.

CHAPTER SIXTEEN

Katie

I awoke suddenly from the dream and felt empty inside. I turned to find that I was in the arms of my husband, Matt. I had been having the same dream about Ben for weeks, and I needed it to end. It was slowly driving me insane. Dreaming about Ben made me feel more alone than ever. I hated it, in fact. It was the last thing that I wanted to do, and I didn't understand why I kept having the same dream. It was a little humiliating, to say the least.

Matt and I had been married now for almost six months. I had expected our marital bliss to last so much longer—why wouldn't it? But things had not been going well between us, and I wasn't sure what to do about it. I couldn't figure out why things were falling apart for us, but it had happened rather quickly. Too quickly. Then the dreams started occurring, and I had to believe it was because my happiness was disappearing. It just made me wonder if I had really made the right decision all those months ago. Maybe I should have chosen Ben and believed in the spark we had. I just hadn't expected my marriage to start falling apart so soon, or ever for that matter. I had every reason to believe that we were a good match, and we loved each other, so what was happening to us?

Matt and I had been happy—blissfully so—for a while, which was why things were so confusing to me. After the wedding, we had gone on our honeymoon and had the time of our lives. It had been one adventure after another, and I had loved every moment I had spent with him. Upon our return, we made arrangements for me to move into his studio apartment, and things were official. We quickly fell into a routine together, and I couldn't have been happier about it.

At first, it had been a little bittersweet for me to leave my own apartment; there were so many memories there. Not to mention it was the first real thing I had of my own, that I had acquired on my own. Selling it was not only a sign of a fresh start for my future, but also an end of an era, and that's what made me sad. I was so used to being on my own, happily independent, and now things were just different.

Despite having to sell my apartment and move in with Matt, I had been ecstatic about the future. Who knew what was in store for us? My business was doing well, and we were newlyweds. Although I had moved into his studio apartment, we weren't planning on staying there. I had always wanted a home of my own, a house to raise a family in. Once we returned, we had started to make arrangements to find the home of our dreams. Matt hired a real estate agent, and the hunt was on.

It didn't take long at all before we had found a great place in the country. It was quite the grand colonial structure, the kind of home I had always dreamed of living in. It even came with a guesthouse in the back so people could come and stay with us and we would still have our own privacy. There were a lot of acres to the property and the backyard was built for entertaining guests. The best part of the home was the studio inside that I could use for my designs. There would be times that I wouldn't have to drive into the city; I could just work from home. I could create without distraction and have my designs come to life in the comfort of my own home.

I lay in bed thinking about when we had moved into our home and how happy we had been together. I felt sad thinking that I may have made a huge mistake. After we had moved into the house, we were blissfully in love for about a month before things started to change between us. I shook my head as I thought about it. Just a month. Maybe I had been a fool after all to get married so quickly, without any thought to how well we really knew each other. Yes, we fell in love quickly, but would that love last a lifetime? I was no longer sure of that.

I wasn't sure exactly when the change had suddenly occurred. One day, things were different. It was a little bizarre. It wasn't as if we'd had a huge fight. Nothing major even happened; things were just different for us.

When I married Matt, I didn't question my love for him. He'd made me happy, and I had wanted to marry him. He was the perfect man, if there was such a thing. He was attentive and kind, and he bent over backward for me. I couldn't dispute the fact that he treated me like a goddess, which was really nice. I never felt scared around him; in fact, he always made me feel safe. Not only that but we had a fulfilling sex life, so things between us certainly had been off to a good start.

We had a good union, and although it wasn't that crazy feeling I used to get with Ben, it was built off something good and pure. It was enough for me—I could have done that my whole life. Yes, life had been pretty spectacular for a while. Unfortunately, those happy feelings didn't stay. I felt sick to my stomach thinking about how we'd gotten to this sad point.

Things had changed so much between Matt and I over the past few months that I found my mind drifting back to Ben and what might have been. I knew it was wrong and that I should be focusing on Matt, but he was really making it hard for me to do so. Matt had changed. I couldn't quite put my finger on it, but there was definitely something off about him. In fact, there were times where I barely recognized the man I had married, and that scared me more than anything. It was too soon for us to be having these kinds of problems in our marriage. Wasn't the honeymoon stage supposed to last a whole year? Matt clearly hadn't gotten that memo because things between us started to change almost immediately.

It made me wonder if Ben had been right when he told me that Matt was just trying to lock me down so he didn't lose me. Could that have been possible? I didn't even want to think about anything like that, and yet Matt had changed drastically since we married. Had it all been an act? Again I couldn't be sure because I couldn't pinpoint when the changes had occurred, which made the situation all the more frightening. How could I have been so wrong about someone I loved so much? My judgment was rarely off when it came to meeting new people. In fact, it was usually on point. There wasn't a time I'd dated someone who I wasn't sure of from the beginning. Yet, I had managed to marry a man that I was beginning to believe I didn't know at all.

Then there was Ben, the man I had always loved. I had turned my back on him because he had seemed such a flake at the time. He couldn't seem to make a decision about us, and it had driven me insane. If only he had come to me long before and expressed his love. Things might have been different. Or maybe it was my fault all along for not accepting his love when he finally did give it to me. I was so torn up inside wondering where I had gone wrong and whether or not I had chosen the right man.

But the fact remained that things had gone sour between Matt and I, and I wasn't sure that it could be reversed. We'd had a perfect marriage together for about a month. We had gone to all sorts of lavish parties and events, giving off the impression that we were the perfect couple, and we were. Or at least I had thought so. Matt often had to make appearances at football games, and I had reveled in the excitement and energy of those games. It had been thrilling to see his life, to learn how his job worked. Together we had made one hell of a great team. Then one day out of the blue everything just changed.

Matt started asking me questions about Ben. At first it had taken me off guard, and then it became worrisome. The questions made him angry, and the answers rarely satisfied him. He wanted to know everything about our relationship even though I had insisted to him that none of it mattered any longer. Matt wanted to know why we had ended our relationship and how long we had been together. He even wanted to know how many times we'd had sex together. I had scoffed at those questions, but it only made him believe I was trying to hide things from him. I couldn't understand his obsession with one of my past lovers; it all seemed to come out of nowhere.

When the questions became too personal, I refused to answer them, which would completely set him off. I insisted that my past with Ben shouldn't matter to him and that he was obsessing over it for nothing. Matt was sure that I was still hung up on my ex, even though I had not seen or heard from Ben since he had shown up at my apartment the night before the wedding. It was madness, and his accusations were starting to eat away at our relationship.

I had begged Matt to drop it all and allow us to be happy without worrying about the past, but he just couldn't seem to let it go. There would be times when he never spoke of it, and I'd think he'd finally let it go, but then it would creep back in and the next thing I knew he would be asking me questions all over again. The process had become exhausting for me. His insecurities over Ben were destroying our marriage.

The badgering from Matt became so hostile that I started canceling event invitations and avoiding galas altogether. I worried that on one of those occasions I would end up running into Ben while I was with Matt and there would be a scene. I couldn't even think of anything more embarrassing, and I wanted to avoid it at all costs. I had seen Ben a few times on the news in the past few months, and his philanthropy crusades were well known in the city. There would be a good chance of running into him if I went to an event. Seeing Ben on the news made me wonder if Matt had seen him around as well. Maybe the fact that Ben was so visible in the media had sparked Matt's curiosity on the subject. It was obvious, however, that my husband didn't trust me one bit, and that was something I had a hard time living with.

In the end, I had been completely honest with Matt about the relationship I'd had with Ben, in the hopes that he would finally be able to let it go. I just wanted us to be happy, and I had hoped that once he knew everything he would come back to me in the way that he used to. Unfortunately, as I had suspected before, it only made the situation worse. I had been trying ever since to make him happy and to forget that there was ever another man. It wasn't like I had cheated on him, so I felt his anger toward the situation was completely unwarranted.

I was waiting for Matt to return home from work. I had some exciting news to share with him, and I hoped that it would change everything between us. That was all I wanted, to get my marriage back on track and have the love of my life back. If things didn't change soon we would be finished. I couldn't live that way. I hadn't done anything wrong, and yet I felt like I was being punished for something.

I was in the kitchen whipping up some salmon with a salad

for dinner when Matt came through the door from work. He stepped into the kitchen, and he smiled warmly when he saw me. It made me feel like maybe things were going to be okay. I always loved his smile, especially when it was directed at me. It looked like we might have a good night after all.

"Katie, you look ravishing. How was your day, my dear?"

I smiled as he came around the kitchen island to kiss me on the lips. "My day was wonderful, thank you. Things are going well in the studio. My new designs are almost ready to showcase, and I was able to get home on time to make my special man a delicious dinner."

He chuckled. "It smells terrific."

He handed me a box, and I looked down at it, confused. "What is it?"

"It's me telling you that I'm sorry. I don't want to lose you, Katie, and I've been a fool lately."

"Matt, you know I love you. I just want things to go back to the way they were. I miss how things were."

"I know. I've just been upset with your involvement with Ben. I thought maybe you wanted him more than me, that you regretted marrying me. I'm worried that you're going to leave me and go back to him. I realized though that it would be my own behavior that caused that. I haven't been very nice to you lately."

Tears started to stream down my face. This is what I had been waiting to hear from him.

"Oh Katie, I'm sorry. Please don't cry. This is all my fault. I'm the one that pushed you away, and I just hope that I can fix things now."

I looked back down at the box and opened it to find a diamond bracelet inside. He wrapped me in his arms and held me tight. We parted for a kiss, and I hoped that this would be a new beginning for us.

"I also have some good news to share with you."

"Oh? And what's that?" He smiled at me with curiosity sparkling in his eyes.

I took a deep breath and said, "I'm pregnant."

Shock marked his face. I almost laughed at the sight of it. He definitely didn't expect that one. He started to laugh along with me. "Wow, you definitely did catch me by surprise with that one."

I hurriedly asked, "But it's okay, right? You're happy?"

"Of course I am, sweetheart. I just didn't expect it that's all. This is wonderful news."

"I love you, Matt. Everything is going to work out just fine."

"I love you too, Katie."

He pulled me in for another hug, and I finally felt safe there again.

CHAPTER SEVENTEEN

Katie

My pregnancy flew by, and it was a little more than I had bargained for. I did everything that I was supposed to do. I ate really well and continued to exercise, but pregnancy was not for the faint of heart. I carried around a little basketball-sized bump under my dress most times and felt blessed that I didn't gain a lot of weight during my pregnancy. I had terrible morning sickness throughout, however, and I was looking forward to it being over with. I wanted to get back to feeling normal instead of feeling sick every single day. All I thought about these days was holding my baby in my arms. A smile came to my face every time I thought about it. I pictured rocking the baby to sleep and feeding the child. I couldn't have been more excited about the prospect of being a mother. It was one of my biggest dreams, and it was finally coming true. I loved Matt will all my heart and we were going to have a blast raising our child together.

Both our families came together and gave me the most incredible shower I could have ever dreamed of. It was more than I had bargained for, but living on the Upper East Side of New York was all about going big on everything. It was something I just had to get used to. We had the shower at the plaza, and it was as elegant as our wedding had been. I felt it was overboard considering it was just a baby shower, but that was just the way things were done, and I was still grateful to have people in my life that loved me that much. I was shocked to find a few hundred people waiting there to celebrate with me—I didn't even know some of them. But they were all there and happy to help celebrate. The gifts had been lavish and much needed. I had barely bought anything myself because I had been so busy keeping the company running.

The nursery was complete, but we hadn't purchased anything to fill it yet. We would have more than we needed for our bundle of joy. With so many people there, I had found the event a little overwhelming, but it was something I got over quickly enough. I had expected a more private affair with just immediate friends and family, but Matt and my best friend had made sure it was nothing like that at all. So I had accepted it, and it turned out to be quite a night, though I was fairly exhausted with the whole thing afterward. It had been one hell of a party, but it was tiring being around all those people. I was pretty sure that our child would have enough clothing to get through to college. After the shower, I had looked through all the clothing, finding them so cute. I hung them lovingly in the closet and some put away in drawers. I was very grateful for everything I had been given, and it caused me an immense amount of excitement at the thought of what was next to come.

I couldn't wait to see our baby and get to use all the things that were given to us. Being around people at the shower made me realize just how excited I was to be a mother and see what that next step in our future was like. I knew that Matt would make a wonderful father, and I looked forward to experiencing that with him. He had changed a lot, and I knew that he really loved me. I was sure that we could get through anything if we just stuck together. That was what was most important.

Since our talk, things had been going really well between Matt and me. I couldn't ask for anything more. He was on his best behavior, and I felt the connection between us growing stronger, and that was all I ever wanted. Matt no longer brought up Ben, and I was grateful for that as well. I didn't want to be punished for someone I had dated in the past. I never wanted to judge him about his past, and I didn't think I should be judged based on anything that happened between Ben and me. It just wasn't right.

Everything was great now between Matt and me, and it made me feel like the trouble between us was a thing of the past. I was so grateful we had resolved our issues because I didn't want to bring our child into the world if things between us weren't good. I wanted that child to be loved as much as possible, not having to come into a home where the parents were constantly fighting. But I felt good about things, and that was all that mattered—I would be okay from then on out. I truly believed that we would be good now and being a family would be an easy step for us. It was all going to be all right—I chanted that often.

The months that passed since that conversation had been nothing short of a whirlwind. We were both as busy as ever. There was so much planning to do to prepare for the baby, plus I still had to juggle the company I ran, and that was no easy task. There was so little time to prepare, and yet the baby was coming sooner rather than later. I hadn't realized how busy I would be with the clothing line I had launched, and being pregnant didn't allow for me to get much done. I had to delegate a lot to my team, but it was probably about time I did that anyway. It just seemed that the company was getting bigger and I didn't have enough hours in the day to complete what I wanted. I liked being part of the whirlwind, and I knew I would miss that part once the baby came. I liked being very hands-on, but I knew I would have to take a step back from that and spend more time in my own studio. Things were just going to be a little crazy for a while. I thrived in that environment though, so I didn't worry too much about it.

I was thrilled that my line was being picked up by some celebrities—it helped immensely in fast-tracking my fashion line. Once a celebrity wore my items everyone wanted them. It was just that easy. Seeing it splashed all over the magazines was like seeing my dreams come true right before my eyes. I couldn't have imagined how well things had been going, and I was grateful for it all—I wouldn't have it any other way. The future looked bright for my line, and I knew I was going to continue to be successful and probably very wealthy because of it. Not that money ever meant much to me, but the success portion always did. I had wanted to be someone, and it looked like it was going to happen exactly the way I had always envisioned it. The more my line soared, the more I was being considered as a designer to be reckoned with. Finally, being able to call myself one of the elite designers was something to be proud of.

I had a long way to go, but I believed I would go all the way to the top in no time. The most exciting part for me was when I decided to start up a couture line for children. I had decided on it as soon as I realized I was pregnant. I wanted to be able to design clothing for my child and then send it out into the world. I had started putting things together while I was pregnant, and seeing the dress and suits I'd created gave me so much pride. I couldn't imagine being happier than I was then. Everything was just the way that I wanted it. As soon as word got out that I was designing clothes for children, I had orders pouring in. We had to hire a whole new team just to handle the children's couture line because we had trouble keeping up with the orders. That was all good news for me, of course. I was widely popular and my line was exclusive only to a few places. I was thinking of opening my own boutique to showcase the children's line and then eventually spreading that chain all over the world. It was a dream of mine but one that would have to wait. I had my hands full already with the baby coming.

Scrambling to keep up with orders was a thing of the past. We were all caught up now and able to handle anything that came our way. The designs were selling as soon as we launched, and I continued to sell out like crazy. I couldn't wait to find out what I was having so I would know whether my child would be sporting my dresses or blazers. Celebrities wanted the first choice, and I had regular clients on waiting lists dying to get my clothing before it hit the stores.

I had a new line available as well, but it would not be launched until I had my little bundle. Things were getting close, and I needed to focus on my pregnancy—too much stress was not good for the baby. Not that I had much to be stressed about. My marriage was back on track, and we had a little one on the way. We were just very busy people.

I needed everything to be right for the new line, but what I needed right now was to focus on Matt and the baby. He was just as excited as I was to meet our little one. I couldn't wait to see his face when the child was born. I knew deep down that he would make a wonderful father.

I was due in a matter of days, and I was anxious to get things over with. It was time to start the new chapter in my life. I couldn't wait to find out what I was having, and sometimes I thought that Matt was even more excited about finding out the sex of the baby than I was, if that was possible. Being pregnant was for the birds—I was over the back aches, weight gain, and vomiting. It was time to get out of this and get some baby love. I had been longing for a glass of wine for months, and soon enough I would be able to partake in a glass or two, which was exactly what I needed. The best part was that Matt and I were having plenty of sex these days to try to induce me. I was desperate to go into labor, and having sex was just a step in the right direction. Unfortunately, it hadn't been working no matter how many different positions and techniques we tried. Whenever I suggested we might need to be a bit rougher, Matt said he didn't want to hurt me or the baby, so pregnant I remained.

The next morning when I woke up, I rolled to the side of the bed feeling like a beached whale. I prayed that I would go into labor that day. I swung my legs over the bed and headed to the bathroom before my bladder burst. I peed so many times during the day no matter what I did to stop it. I went to the bathroom and started to brush my teeth. Matt had already gone off to work for the day, and all I could think about was going back to bed. I was exhausted and needed more rest. I considered going out to sit by our pool if it wasn't too hot out. A cool swim would probably make me feel better.

I started brushing my teeth, and suddenly I felt a pop and water pooled down at my feet. I put a hand between my legs and gasped. My water had broken, and suddenly I felt panicky. I had thought it would be more dramatic, like a flood, but it was more like a trickle down my leg. I didn't know what to do; my mind went suddenly blank. I dropped the toothbrush and headed back into the bedroom to find my phone. I immediately called Matt and told him that I was in labor. He told me he would send a driver for me and meet me at the hospital as soon as he could. I grabbed my hospital bag and headed for the door to wait for the driver to arrive.

CHAPTER EIGHTEEN

Katie

I was spent. I couldn't remember a time that I had felt so exhausted. Labor had been quite an experience and one that no one could ever prepare you for. I had read the books and even watched the videos. Friends and family had told me what to expect, but despite all their advice and the research I had conducted myself, it was still nothing like I had ever imagined. It was worse, far worse. An exhausting labor that was the worst pain I had ever experienced. My labor itself wasn't that long, but those five hours had been long enough—it had felt like an eternity of pain. The contractions had ripped through me without any mercy. I couldn't imagine it being any worse, and yet it had gone on for hours on end. I had believed in a drug-free labor, and I had got my money's worth. I had felt it was the best decision for me and the baby, but the downside was that I felt everything. It had truly been the longest five hours of my life. Thank god there had been a benefit to the whole thing in the end. I wondered though how people had five kids—I couldn't imagine going through that so many times. It was almost barbaric.

Thankfully I had a private suite, compliments of my loving husband. It was luxurious and felt like a home away from home. I loved the fact that I had my privacy in such a time. The suite I was staying in was just as big as my master bedroom in the colonial house we now owned. It had everything that I could possibly need to make myself comfortable. There was a flat-screen TV, though I had yet to use it. The suite resembled an actual bedroom to make guests feel right at home. I had packed my overnight bag with necessities from home, so I had everything that I needed.

Matt had shown up to the hospital right on time and held my hand during the labor. When the baby had finally come out, it was a beautiful baby girl. I had been overjoyed, picturing the darling little thing wearing the precious dresses from my line. I would dote on the girl and make her feel like a true princess. Looking down into her little eyes for the first time had completed my life. I couldn't imagine needing anything more in life now that I had my precious little girl. When I had reluctantly handed the child over to Matt, he had looked down at her in awe, a truly endearing sight. He had fallen in love at first sight with our daughter and had agreed to name her Bella. Little Bella was a true representation of our love for one another.

We had a staff of nurses that came in frequently to help out and check on little Bella. It made things so much easier for me as I recovered. I wasn't planning on breastfeeding because my schedule would not allow for it, and we would have a nanny at the house to help out anyway. I would need to get back into the office as soon as possible, and because of that, I would have to be flexible with feedings.

I lay there in bed reading and waiting for Matt to arrive. I was famished and he promised to bring me in some food. I was still very sore from the labor, so I didn't move around as much as I would have liked. I considered flipping on the TV but instead decided to read for a little while. Bella was in the nursery getting a checkup from the doctors, and I missed her already. She would need to have a bath when I came back to the room, and I wanted to be the one to do it.

I loved being hands-on with Bella and knew that having a nanny would be difficult for me. I had a hard time delegating for my company; how much harder would it be to delegate to a nanny with my own child? It wasn't going to be easy, but Matt insisted on having a nanny, as he'd grown up with one and felt it was essential, especially if I wanted to go back to work. There were times that I felt Matt would prefer if I stayed at home and didn't work at all. I knew he was immensely proud of me for all my achievements, but he felt it was unnecessary for me to work because he was already wealthy. I didn't care about money, of course. I just wanted to have something to call my own.

I had worked hard to get the company to where it was, and I adored fashion. I knew I would go slowly insane if I were to be a stay-at-home mom. I wanted to be more than just a wife and mother. Running a fashion line defined me, and it was my own unique mark on the world. How could I want anything less than that? I could still be a mother and a wife with my company—the three fulfilled me more than anything ever could. It was what I wanted, and although I didn't agree with having a nanny, I would accept the help if it meant that Matt would be okay with me having my own career as well. Maybe he was a little old-fashioned. I had never really thought of him in that way, but it was obvious he liked things a certain way. Since I didn't really care one way or another, I just let things slide off my shoulders. It wasn't enough to worry about after all.

I had read about two chapters when Matt walked through the door holding Bella. I smiled knowing he must have gone to the nursery as soon as he entered the hospital. I loved seeing our sweet bundle in his arms; they looked so cute together. He came to the side of the bed and bent down so that I could see Bella. She was sleeping and her sweet face was rosy and just darling. I looked up at him. "Was the doctor finished with her? Everything's okay?"

"Yes, she's as fit as can be. I managed to snatch her up before they could put her back to bed. So she's ours for the time being." He looked down at Bella. "My god, she's as beautiful as you are, Katie."

"Can I hold her?" I held out my arms, and Matt placed her gently in them. I nuzzled into the neck of the little one and kissed the top of her head. She had that sweet baby scent to her, and I loved breathing it in. It was intoxicating and I loved my little one more than I could ever have imagined.

"Yes, you are right, she's very beautiful, but I can't take all the credit for it."

"Well, maybe I had some help in it, but she looks just like you, my love."

Matt bent down and kissed me on the forehead as I nuzzled our daughter. Everything was just perfect—I couldn't ask for a single thing more in my life.

"Bella is just the perfect name. I'm glad you decided to use it. It suits her just fine."

I smiled. "Thank you. I love it as well. She looks just like a Bella."

The door to my suite opened and a nurse walked in with a package. Both Matt and I turned to watch as she came toward us. It was one of those "It's A Girl" baskets filled with all kinds of goodies. It was beautiful and it was tied perfectly with a pink balloon. I smiled as the nurse set it down on the table.

"It looks like another package arrived for little Bella. I will just leave it here."

"Oh, Bella is getting spoiled rotten to be sure."

The nurse smiled. "She's one lucky little girl." She turned and left the room, leaving us alone once again. I looked at the basket from afar, unable to move with the baby in my arms. I watched as Matt went over to look at the basket. I was excited to see what was inside. It looked rather elaborate.

"Who is it from?"

"Not sure." He looked around for a card to see who had sent the grand package. It was obvious that a lot of money had been spent on the basket, and I wondered who would go to that kind of trouble. It had to have been someone who hadn't attended the shower, and I didn't know who that would be.

"There isn't a card?"

"No. Oh, wait. There's a note. There isn't a name on it anywhere though. Who would send such a package and not say who it's from? That's a little weird, isn't it?" His brow furrowed, and I tried to think of who would send the package.

"Yeah, it is a little weird. I wasn't expecting anything today. I've been getting some flowers, but that's about it. I can't imagine who would send that package."

Matt was looking inside the package, and I found it weird that he hadn't brought the basket to me to look at yet. He was just rummaging through it as if looking for something. His behavior was just as bizarre as the mystery package.

"The things inside this basket are very expensive. Very expensive. I don't understand why such an expensive gift would come with no card? How are we supposed to thank this person?"

"Can I see the basket, Matt? I would like to see what's inside as well."

He ignored me as he continued looking inside the basket. I was becoming annoyed as I watched him. He wasn't even paying attention to the beautiful things inside; he was just sorting through it as if looking for a clue. I couldn't imagine what had come over him, but he was irritating me. I wanted to look at the package myself and see what there was for Bella. From afar the items looked quite chic, and I knew there was an outfit or two in there.

He suddenly turned toward me, and his gaze narrowed. Confused, I just stared back at him trying to understand why he suddenly looked angry. I had never seen someone so worked up over a baby basket. Maybe the stress of work was starting to get to him. I wasn't sure what it was, but I wasn't in the mood for weird behavior. I just wanted to look at the basket.

"The basket is from him, isn't it?"

My brow furrowed. "Who are you referring to?"

"Don't act dumb, Katie. You know exactly who I'm talking about."

"Excuse me? Actually, I have no idea why you've decided to suddenly have a temper tantrum. What has you so upset?"

He just stared at me, and I grew angry. I looked down at Bella and decided to let the anger go. He was itching for a fight, and I had no idea why. I wasn't going to fall for it though and fight in front of Bella. The little thing was sleeping, and I wasn't going to do anything to change that.

"Can I please see the basket? It looks beautiful and I want to see what's inside."

"Are you actually going to lay there and pretend that you have no idea who sent the package?"

My mouth dropped open. I could not believe what I was hearing. He looked pissed at me, and I couldn't imagine why. How would I know who sent the package? I'd learned of its existence at the exact same time he had. He was behaving irrationally, and I didn't like the look of it. It reminded me of the old days when we used to fight. I had thought we were over that, but maybe it had all been an act.

"What is the matter with you?" Tears collected in my eyes, and I didn't know what was going on.

"This is from Ben, isn't it? I should have known as soon as I saw it."

I laughed, not knowing what else I could do at that point. "You must be kidding me? How the hell would I know who sent it, Matt? I'm as puzzled as you are. As far as Ben goes, I haven't spoken to the man since before the wedding. If he sent the basket, I'm certainly unaware of it."

He snorted. "If I didn't know better, I might have to start wondering if Bella is even my child."

I gasped. I sat there speechless as shock coursed through me. I stared at Matt as tears streamed down my cheeks. I felt humiliated and betrayed. How could my own husband say something so foul to me? I was appalled by his words. I could barely find the words to tell him off. "You have no right to talk to me in that manner. Seriously, Matt, what the hell is wrong with you?"

He shook his head slowly and threw his hands up in the air. He stormed from the room without looking back at me.

"Matt," I called out after him.

There was no answer, and he didn't return to the room. I sat there shocked, unable to process what had happened in the past few minutes. His words had been monstrous, and all over a mystery basket. I had no idea if the basket came from Ben, but even if it did, it didn't warrant the kind of reaction I got from Matt. Shock made a home inside of me as I tried to process his words. I couldn't believe he had the nerve to suggest that Bella was not his child. To suggest that it was Ben's was a little more than I could take. He deserved to have his eyes clawed out for that behavior, but instead, he had marched out without even talking things through with me. Who was the man I had married?

It seemed like we were back at square one. As soon as Ben

was mentioned, Matt seemed to lose all sense of himself. I hadn't seen Ben in over a year, and yet we were still fighting about him. Matt was a completely different person when it came to Ben, and I didn't like that person at all. I wasn't sure what I was going to do about the situation, but Matt's words were unforgivable.

I looked down at Bella, feeling suddenly very sad and lonely. The poor thing had no idea about adult concerns. What an innocent world she lived in, for the time being at least. I rocked little Bella and wondered how I had gotten myself into the mess that I was in. I thought my marriage was okay, but apparently, there was something really wrong with it. What had happened to our lovely life? I knew that I couldn't go back to fighting like that with Matt. I slid off the bed carefully and brought Bella to the bassinet and laid her down gently. She could sleep comfortably while I took a look at that package. I was still very much curious as to what was inside of it.

I started to pick through the package, marveling at the beautiful things inside. There was a literal silver spoon and some beautiful designer dresses. I smiled as I looked through the basket wondering at the elaborateness of it all. There was a tiny pair of diamond stud earrings in there for a baby. I had planned on getting the little one's ears pierced in a few months, but what a gift. Who would go to all this trouble? Could it really have been Ben that sent it? After all this time, would he do such a thing? Whoever sent it certainly had a lot of money to burn. I was smiling from ear to ear when I heard a familiar voice behind her.

"I'm glad you like the basket."

I froze and then spun around to find Ben behind me. Just like the first time I met him, my heart slammed against my chest in the most wondrous way. It had been him all along. He had sent the package, had thought about me—after all this time he was still thinking about me. I remembered the last time that I saw him in my apartment, and I realized that after all this time I still loved him. That thought made me sad because I had tried so hard to be a part of another life, and that life was now spiraling out of control. I didn't understand Matt's reaction toward me all the time when I was honestly trying to have a happy life with him. But maybe he sensed that all along my heart had never truly been his completely. There had always been a piece of it somewhere else.

"What are you doing here, Ben? This is a bad idea. If Matt saw you here, I would be filling out divorce papers for sure." Tears built up in my eyes and spilled down my cheeks.

A shocked look came over his face, and he was by my side in a second. He wrapped his arms around me and hugged me tight.

"What's wrong, Katie? I didn't come here to cause you any problems. I'm sorry, that wasn't my intention, and I had no idea that it would have that kind of effect on you. This is a happy day. You have a new daughter—you shouldn't be crying."

"It's Matt. He saw the package that you sent and he went insane. He despises you, and he knows about our past. He stormed out of here, but he could be back any minute. If he saw you here, it would be bad on an epic scale. You have no idea."

Ben's eyes grew stormy. "What are you talking about? Why would your husband behave like that? I thought you said he was a kind man—he certainly doesn't sound like it to me."

Suddenly I started sobbing. My feelings about Matt just poured out of me. I felt helpless and confused by the way that Matt treated me when it came to Ben.

"Dear god. I had no idea, Katie. I should have sent the package with a name, but I thought it was best not to. I fully intended on speaking to Matt if he were here and congratulating him. I feel no ill will for the man, until now of course. I don't understand why he's acting so outrageously. He won, I lost. I haven't tried to contact you until now, and that was a mistake. I'm sorry. I didn't send it to cause problems. I just wanted to congratulate you on the baby."

I looked up at him and felt my heart beat hard all over again. He had that power over me even after all this time. I didn't know what to do about that feeling. "He will hate me if he knows you are here."

"He won't know. I wasn't sure how Matt would react if I came up, so I had someone watch the building. I will know he's coming before he even steps foot in the hospital. You have nothing to worry about. Please, you need to stop crying."

"What are you doing here, Ben? You could have called or sent a message. You didn't need to come to the hospital."

"I just wanted to see you and your new daughter. Is that so terrible?"

"How did you know that I had a girl?"

"I have my hand in a lot of things, Katie. I like to know things. I just needed to know that you were happy and well taken care of. It's important to me."

"Well, it hasn't been easy. We've had some problems." Why did I always feel the need to bare my soul to Ben? He didn't need to know any more about my marital problems than I'd already told him, but my mouth just wouldn't listen to my brain.

"Newlyweds shouldn't have any problems. Not big ones anyway. He shouldn't be leaving you alone at the hospital."

"You don't understand. He is obsessed with our past, and he thinks I still have feelings for you. He can't get over it."

"He doesn't deserve you."

"And you do?"

He shrugged, and I suddenly felt bad. "I'm sorry. We don't have to be difficult about this. Matt is a good guy. Our relationship has had its bumps because he's jealous of you. I don't know why he's obsessed with you."

Ben walked to the bassinet and took a look inside. He grinned as he looked down at Bella. "She's a beauty, Katie. No big surprise there."

I was shocked to see him bend down and scoop Bella up into his arms. I thought he might feel weird about holding another man's child, but he seemed very comfortable with Bella in his arms.

"What's her name?"

"Bella."

He chuckled. "What a tiny little thing. It's amazing."

They looked so cute together that it brought fresh tears to my eyes. I gulped down a lump in my throat and said something that I knew I shouldn't say. "I picked the wrong guy, didn't I? I made the wrong choice. I loved him, but I shouldn't have married him."

Ben looked up at me with surprise on his face. He pursed his lips and then looked back down at Bella. He gently set her down in the bassinet and slowly walked over to me.

"This is not your fault, Katie. If anything, it's mine. I waited too long before I told you how I felt, and that was wrong. How could I possibly be mad when you finally chose someone else? I fucked up, not you."

He wrapped his arms around me once again and hugged me tightly. I sobbed into his chest, feeling hopeless about everything.

"It was not my intention to upset you today. I'm sorry. I just needed to see you."

Ben's phone rang and he looked at the message, then clicked it off suddenly. He pulled away from me. "Enjoy your baby, Katie. She is the best reason in the world to be happy." He bent down and kissed me on the lips, and I felt complete again, like he had never left. He turned from me then and left the room so quickly that it was hard to believe he was ever there in the first place. I glanced at the basket and took a deep sigh. I returned to my bed, wiping away at my tears, trying to find my composure.

A few minutes later, Matt walked through the suite door, surprising me. He had flowers in his hand and a sheepish look on his face. I almost laughed at the sight of him. So, that was why Ben had left so quickly. The ringing phone had been a notification that Matt had arrived back at the hospital. I was thankful he left in time because I couldn't even imagine what Matt would have done had he found Ben in my room. He would have assumed that I had been seeing him all along.

"Katie, I am sorry for the way I reacted."

I put my hands up to block him from touching me. "Oh, please, don't you dare. You don't get to speak to me the way you did and then come back here with flowers like everything's going to be okay."

He stood there and stared at me in shock. He had never heard me speak to him that way. I didn't care. I would not be spoken to in that way by someone who was supposed to cherish me.

"If you can't get a handle on that jealousy, I will leave you."

I closed my eyes, and that ended the conversation. I needed to get some rest before Bella awoke again.

CHAPTER NINETEEN

Katie

Six months went by, and I was once again getting ready for another AIDS benefit. It was my first real event since I had Bella, and I was really looking forward to it. I loved getting dressed up and going out. I had been in baby mode for months, and it was about time I got back out there and made an impression on my life. Benefits were important to me, and I wanted to be a part of that life once again. I had lost the baby weight, and I bought a beautiful lace gown that I was dying to wear. I knew I would look smoking hot in it, and I was excited to get ready for the event. It was all I could think about, in fact.

Matt had actually purchased the dress for me, and it was a nice gesture. It had been a long time since we had been out together. We had been immersed in Bella, which was also a good thing, but now it was time for me to get back out in the world. Matt had also been working a lot, so it was hard to get out and have a date. He often came home late at night and went straight to bed. He was a busy guy, and that was sometimes hard for us as well, but I tried to be understanding because I knew he was trying to provide a good life for us.

After what had happened at the hospital some six months ago, things seemed to be okay between us again. Things were just like I wanted them to be. But I was never sure if his bad side was going to creep up again. I thought it was behind us; that was, until we had gone out one night for a few drinks. Once Matt had a few in him, he had gone on about Ben again. It was actually becoming quite exhausting for me. It made me feel like giving up and washing my hands of the whole thing. I wanted to keep my family together for Bella's sake and because I still loved Matt, but I didn't want to have the same argument for the rest of my life.

After that last fight, I saw less and less of Matt. In fact, for the past few months, I had only seen him a few days a week. The rest of the time, he came home so late I was already sleeping. When he was home, he often went to his office. It had gotten to the point where I would bring Bella to his office so the child had some time with her father. Whatever was going on between us, Matt seemed to forget that there was another person involved, someone that needed him too. Bella was more important than his work; it wasn't like we were strapped for cash or anything.

I looked up as Matt came into our bedroom and looked me over as I stood there adorned in my new gown. He looked as handsome as ever in a tuxedo, ready for the event as well. I often forgot how handsome he was, as I rarely saw him these days. I had fallen in love with him not so long ago, and I worried that it was all falling apart. I didn't want that, but I felt that it was now out of my control.

He walked up to me and kissed me on the cheek. "You look absolutely stunning, Katie. What a dress. I knew it would look amazing on you."

I smiled. "Thank you."

He hugged me tight. "I'm really looking forward to having you on my arm tonight, my dear. Especially since you look so beautiful. It's certainly been a while for us."

I smiled sadly, understanding more than he did.

"I hope you understand that I'm just trying to provide us with the best possible life."

I shook my head. "We already have a good life. You're doing something else. Your family needs you, your daughter needs you, and that's more important. You're the owner—you should be able to let someone else run it and be here with us."

He nodded. "You're right. I'm sorry."

THE AIDS BENEFIT was being held at one of the most elite hotels in the city. The dining room alone was to die for. I had been there to dine on more than one occasion, and the food was exquisite. I smiled as soon as I walked into the hotel, feeling good about being out again. I was very blessed to have the life I did and grateful that I could be a part of benefits such as this. It was quite the lifestyle. Tickets to the AIDS benefit ran a thousand dollars each, but it was all for charity, so I didn't mind the cost. I knew I would never have the time to go back to a place like Africa and invest lengthy time there to work with my hands, so events such as this one were the next best thing.

When we arrived, I spotted the pop star who had become my first celebrity client, and I smiled at the sight of her. She was very much pregnant, and she waved at me when she spotted me. She would be after the couture line as soon as the baby popped, if not sooner. The pop star made a beeline for me and hugged me tightly.

"Katie, you look stunning. You must tell me how you got the baby weight off."

"Oh, it wasn't easy, let me tell you." I smiled, proud of my accomplishment.

"I have heard amazing things about your couture children's line. I must have it when this little one pops out. I'm going to wait until we find out what we're having, and then I will be putting in an order."

"Of course. Just let me know. I'm surprised you're waiting to find out."

She giggled. "I know. I wanted to find out right away, but my man insists on waiting. I can't believe it myself—I think he just likes torturing me. But either way, I will be all over the junior line of yours."

"That's wonderful. You have been one of my most loyal clients. I really do appreciate it."

"Oh please, you are insanely talented. Your clothing is a work of art. I would be foolish not to grab it when I can."

I thanked her again and excused myself from the conversation. I wanted to make sure that my assistant sent a gift basket to the pop star for her baby shower. I liked adding little touches like that for my best clients.

As Matt and I made our way to our table, we were approached by Ben. I had wondered if he was going to be at the event, as he usually found his way to these sorts of things. I was surprised, however, that he had the balls to approach us, but he may have felt safe since there were a lot of people around. I refused to have a scene at the event, however, so I plastered a smile on my face and vowed to be polite. I just hoped that Matt would do the same thing.

"Hello, Matt, Katie, how are you both? I'm glad to see you here. I bet it brings you back to Africa, doesn't it?"

I smiled warmly. "Yes, I think about it often. I would love to go back one day, but it's not in the foreseeable future I'm afraid. Maybe when Bella is old enough to come with me, it would be a wonderful lesson for her."

Ben nodded. "Indeed. You should have brought little Bella. I would have loved to have met her."

I nodded. "Not at this age. It probably wouldn't be much fun for anyone. Babies and benefits don't typically go together."

Ben chuckled. "Yes, I guess you're right."

I periodically glanced at Matt while I talked with Ben. He didn't once speak or even break into a smile. He just stared hard at Ben, and I hoped to god he wasn't going to say something awful. I grew more annoyed as the conversation continued. Why couldn't he just smile or be amiable? Would that be so terrible? He could at least be polite, show me that he had put things about Ben behind him. Our future depended on it, and yet there he was acting like a stone wall, not doing anything normal.

Ben turned to Matt. "I've noticed that your team is doing quite well out there these days. Congratulations, you must be one hell of an owner."

I looked at Matt to see how he was going to handle the situation, and I was shocked to see him glaring at Ben. Oh dear, he was going to make a scene, and that was the last thing I wanted or needed. I just wanted to enjoy myself for one evening without any drama. If the night went badly, I knew that I would hear about Ben on the way home, and I dreaded having that talk for the hundredth time.

"I have stayed quiet long enough, Ben, and I think it's about time that I make myself perfectly clear to you once and for all. I want you to stay the hell away from my family. You have no reason in the world to need to talk to Katie, and I want it to stop immediately." Matt practically hissed out the words, spittle coming out of his mouth.

I gasped, shocked by his words, my face burning with embarrassment. Ben just stared at Matt, his mouth a thin line. I could just imagine what was going through his head. I took a deep breath and turned to Matt.

"What are you doing? You are acting completely untoward. Ben has been nothing but polite to us this evening."

Matt turned to me, and he didn't appear as if he was about to back down for a minute. I didn't like the look he had in his eyes. He was certainly angry, and just the sight of him was causing me heaps of embarrassment. I felt humiliated that the man I had married was behaving in such a way in front of Ben. What must he think of me and my choices to look at me that way?

"What I find interesting, Katie, is that you defend Ben every chance you get. Now, why is that, do you think?"

I looked at him, appalled. What the hell was the matter with him? I looked at Ben and saw that he was biting his tongue in a big way. He took a deep breath and nodded to the both of us. "If you two will excuse me, I think I need a drink."

I watched Ben walk toward the bar, and then I turned to Matt. "How could you behave in that way? After all the talks we've had about Ben, you think it's okay to behave this way? How am I ever going to be able to deal with this? It's too much."

He rolled his eyes. "Please don't start with me, Katie. I'm not in the mood. The guy had a lot of nerve walking up to us, don't you think?"

I shook my head. "He was just being polite, and it's okay for me to speak with the man in social settings without you pitching a fit. Ben and I were together almost two years ago. Two years! It wasn't even a long-term relationship—it was over before I knew it. You are behaving like a fool over someone that I dated a lifetime ago. When are you going to grow up?"

I didn't wait for a response from him; I turned and walked away from him. I needed some time to clear my head. I was disgusted by his behavior, and I required some immediate distance from him. Things weren't getting better between us, that much was obvious. He was never going to be able to let go of his feelings about Ben, and those thoughts were destroying us. We were going to continue to have these same fights endlessly, and I didn't think that I could bear it any longer.

I headed to the bar, wanting a drink as well, and I longed to down a few shots. I wouldn't, of course, but I couldn't help feeling that way. When I sidled up to the bar, Ben was still there, and even though I had no right to be, I was annoyed with him.

"I just can't seem to get rid of you, can I, Ben?"

"It's not like you to be mean, Katie. I'm sorry for approaching you. I keep making mistakes around you, it seems."

I ordered a glass of wine and sipped at it before finally turning to him. "Yeah, saying hi probably wasn't the best idea. But it's not your fault. You were just trying to be nice, and I couldn't control Matt's behavior even if I wanted to."

"I guess I'm just a nice guy," he said, laughing.

"Let's not get ahead of yourself there. You're not really that nice."

He chuckled, but he sounded sad. "Yeah, you're probably right about that one."

"Matt's pretty pissed at me. God, I don't know how we're going to salvage this night. But I probably should go and find him and try to talk to him."

"I'm sorry to have to tell you this, Katie, but Matt left."

"Excuse me?" I said as I took a sip of wine. I felt panicky, and suddenly fear started to crawl up my spine as I tried to understand what Ben was saying to me.

"Yes, I'm afraid your husband has left the event. I was watching you guys argue after I left, and as soon as you walked away from him, he left the party. My driver told me he walked right out to his car, but he never came back in."

"You're lying to me. Why are you saying this?"

"I'm not lying. He left you again. He keeps leaving you."

I stared at him in shock. He couldn't be right. I would not believe that my husband would abandon me at an event, leaving me with no way to get home. He just wouldn't do something like that to me. I took out my phone and dialed his number. The phone rang for a while and then finally went to voice mail. My stomach dropped and I didn't know what to say. Matt never ignored my phone calls, not ever. He never shut off his phone, especially if we were out somewhere together. He was deliberately ignoring me, and I couldn't believe it. What had come over him? He always kept his phone on just in case we got separated. I tried the number again, and it once again went to voice mail.

I looked up at Ben, who was watching me, and my face burned with embarrassment. My husband really had walked out on me and left me at an event alone. I would have to call for a driver, and that was just the shittiest thing for Matt to have done to me. He didn't even say goodbye to me; he had just walked out. I was in shock when I took a seat at the bar. I was clearly not going anywhere anytime soon. I couldn't believe my miserable luck. It really took very little to set Matt off these days.

I gulped my glass of wine and quickly ordered another one. I decided to take it easy on the second one so that I wouldn't get kicked out of the event. I turned to Ben and made a poor attempt at smiling at him. He knew my husband was behaving like a jerk, and it made me feel stupid that he constantly saw Matt at his worst.

"You are gorgeous tonight, if that makes you feel any better."

I chuckled. I knew he was trying to cheer me up, and I appreciated it. I had a hard time smiling, however. All I wanted to do was get my hands on Matt and strangle the life out of him. Matt just kept on disappointing me, and I didn't understand why he couldn't let go and be the husband that I needed. Instead, he continued to be a buffoon. It was embarrassing, to say the least.

"Well, I guess it can't hurt being stunning when your heart is breaking. At least I have something." I finished my drink and motioned to the bartender to bring me another.

"That's a lot of wine in a short period of time, Katie. I know you're upset, but don't get carried away."

"I don't need you to tell me what to do. I already have one husband that does that."

"True, but I assure you that getting wasted is not going to make this situation any better. You need to deal with it, once and for all. You need to face it head on, and you can't do that if you are drunk or hungover. You're better than that, Katie."

I looked over at him and felt grateful that he was looking out for me. But wasn't that what he always did? He was always there, even in the background, watching out for me. "Can you please take me somewhere else? I can't be here right now at this place, and I can't go home right now. I don't want to see Matt."

He looked at me and held my gaze before saying, "Are you sure that's really what you want?"

"Yes, absolutely. I can't be here right now. I have to get out of here."

He grasped my hand, and I followed him out of the main dining area. I hadn't even had a bite to eat of the exquisite meal that was to be served that evening. Everything had spiraled out of control, and my head was still spinning from it all. I felt foolish every time I thought of Matt, and I wanted to be anywhere but there. Somewhere that could allow me a few moments to think of something else.

I was pretty sure that my marriage was over. I couldn't stay married to a man that was bound and determined to make me miserable. Leaving me alone at an event that we had gone to together was just too sickening to think about. Did he even love me at all? What was I supposed to say to the other guests about his rapid departure? It was foolish and I was tired of feeling the way that I did.

"Can you wait here a moment?" I stood outside the door to the dining room and waited while Ben disappeared.

CHAPTER TWENTY

Katie

It wasn't long before Ben returned to my side. "Are you ready?" I nodded. "Okay, let's go."

I couldn't be sure why I was following Ben; it just felt like the right thing to do. I had made so many mistakes in my life, and I just wanted to do something right for once. Being around Ben felt real, and that was what I needed. I had no idea where he was taking me, but I was relieved to be out of the event. It had felt suffocating in there, and I couldn't stand to be around people at that point. Matt had not returned any of my calls, and the more I thought about it, the angrier I got. How dare he treat me in that manner? I didn't deserve it, and I wasn't going to put up with it any longer.

I followed Ben to the elevator, and he pressed the button. He must have had a room in the hotel; he often did that during an event instead of driving all the way back to his own home. When the elevator opened, we stepped inside and he pressed the button for the penthouse suite. We rode up to the most luxurious suite in the entire hotel. I looked over at Ben and was unsure of how I felt at that moment. I couldn't be sure of what would happen once we got up to the suite, but I lacked the ability to care. I was pissed at Matt, and I knew I would have to deal with him eventually, but as far as I was concerned, we were finished. I could no longer continue living that way, and Matt clearly had no intention of changing at all. I had given him more than enough chances to move on from my past and make me happy, and he continued to blow those chances every single time.

When the elevator doors opened, I looked around the penthouse, appreciating it for its value. It was a gorgeous suite, and I liked the way it was laid out. Ben came up behind me, and he gently put his mouth on my shoulder, causing chills to go up my spine. I turned around to face him and kissed him full on the mouth. Our tongues molded together with heat building up between us. I moaned, aching in every part of my body for him. It felt like we had never been apart.

He kissed my mouth, my chin, and lingered on my neck, nipping his way down. He was setting fire to every part of me.

"Please, I need you now. Please don't make me wait."

He picked me up and carried me to the master bedroom. I noticed the room had items scattered around.

"Have you been staying here?"

"No, but I had hoped you would end up here with me, and I wanted to claim you as mine."

"Really? You planned to have me here?" I was shocked.

"Well, I didn't think Matt would make it quite so easy, but yes, I did intend on making you mine again, in body, if not in mind."

"I missed you, Ben."

"God, darling, I missed you too."

"It looks like you have something rough in store for me."

"Well, I think you've been bad, darling, keeping me away

from your beautiful pussy for so long. I haven't stopped thinking about you in two years."

"Bad?"

"Yes, and you need to be punished. A good, hard fucking should make you see where you belong."

I couldn't believe how wet I was getting just from him talking to me. I began to undress, sliding the straps of my lace gown off my shoulders and letting the gown fall to the floor. I was completely nude underneath the dress, and I smiled as he looked me over. He undressed, showing me a completely rock-hard cock ready to punish me just the way that he wanted.

He led me to the bed and bent me over, holding both of my arms behind me back, holding me down. I knew he was going to take me from behind. He picked up a paddle and slapped my bottom with it. I gasped and swore I could cum just like that.

"You're mine, Katie."

I moaned loudly, loving his words.

"Say it. Tell me your mine."

"I'm yours, Ben. I'm all yours. Take me."

He paddled my ass again and drove his cock into me. I cried out, and he plunged in deeper and deeper every time. I was moaning so loudly that I'm sure he was losing his mind. He always used to tell me it was the best sound in the world.

I didn't know how much I could take, and I came all over his cock. He flipped me over, putting his hands around my throat, and my voice caught just as he plunged his cock into me. I got completely foggy and light-headed. I thought I would pass out. He released my throat, pumping inside me hard and fast. I came so hard my whole body rocked.

"Oh Ben, you feel so good. I can't stand it."

"Oh baby, you are perfect. Every part of you. You are so wet. I need to be inside you all the time."

I came again, feeling completely taken by this man. I didn't know if I could ever leave his side again. He had stayed with me for years. Just waiting for me.

"Mmmm baby, I've been thinking about you fucking me all day."

"I missed you so much."

"God, you are dripping so much." He whispered in my ear, his voice husky. His words were only for me. My mouth found his hot and wanting. Our tongues tangled together, and I gasped at the taste of him. My pussy was throbbing for his cock, and I couldn't understand the power he had over my body. He made me ache to be fucked by him.

His hands were on my breasts, kneading them, and I moaned when he pinched one of my nipples. My hand reached behind him and grabbed his ass, and I squeezed it hard thinking about what his powerful thrusts could do to me. He moved inside of me flawlessly, and I moaned with every thrust. He kissed my lips and then moved down to my jaw line and then my neck. He pumped his cock into me rhythmically, making my pussy wetter. He bit my neck, and it caused me to grip him tighter around the waist.

"Oh baby, your cock is so big."

"You like that, don't you darling. You like being fucked by my big cock?"

"Oh yes. Please fuck me harder."

With that, I got exactly what I asked for. He pounded against me over and over again, his cock buried deep inside of me. He was so deep that I could feel his balls slapping up against me.

"Oh god, that feels good. Oh baby, you fuck me so good."

I knew that I was going to cum again, hard—it was inevitable. He was pounding my pussy so good. It was a hard, rough fuck—just what I needed after being without him for so long. I was powerless against his thrusts because he held my arms back so that I was constantly pressed against him. I felt the buildup coming inside of me. My pussy tightened around his cock as he continued to pound against my ass.

I cried out as I exploded on his cock.

"Oh baby, oh baby, I'm cumming."

He slowed his pumping down and released one of my hands. His fingers found my clit, and I moaned as he rubbed hard against it. Everything was ultrasensitive after my orgasm, so the sensation was thrilling.

He slid out of me and pulled me up with my other hand. I was a little out of sorts from my orgasm, but I followed him as he led me to the dresser. He pushed me up against it, and I braced myself against the top. I bent over, my ass pointed in the air. I heard him groan, though it wasn't so much a groan as it was a growl. He couldn't wait to fuck me again, and he made me aware of that when he plunged inside me once again. He went in deep, and the hardness of his cock left me immobilized. He was incredibly gifted with the length and girth of his cock, and every inch of him was filling me up to perfection.

"Fuck me, baby. Fuck me hard."

A little roughness never hurt anyone, and I was so beyond horny at that point that I just wanted him to bury himself in me deep and fuck me hard again.

He pounded inside of me, and I turned around to look at him. He was an incredibly handsome man. And god, that body, so hard and sculpted. It was like he had been photoshopped—he was that perfect to look at. I watched him as he fucked me, and the sight of him pounding into me drove me insane. I came again onto his cock, and I cried out with pleasure.

"You feel so good, baby. Your pussy is so nice and tight. You feel incredible."

"I need your cock, baby. God you feel good."

"You want my cum, baby? You want me to pump your pussy full of cum?"

I moaned eagerly, and he thrust inside of me harder and faster as I felt myself losing control. He cried out as well when he spilled inside of me. He slowed down his thrusts and rubbed my clit slowly, and it felt as luxurious as it always did. I kissed the top of his head, trying to catch my breath.

We moved to the bed, then lay there for an hour, not speaking but just holding each other tight. I wasn't sure what was going to happen next. I didn't know what was right and what was wrong anymore. All my decisions had still led to that moment there with Ben. That moment where I knew I could never go back. It had always been Ben. He had stood by me no matter what my decisions were, while my husband sabotaged every moment we had together with jealousy.

I had thought having the baby would have completed our family and killed all the jealousy, but it hadn't. He had allowed his jealousy to poison our relationship to the point where he was hardly at home to even see his daughter. I knew I couldn't live like that anymore. I knew that I had put my fair share of effort into the relationship and shouldn't feel any guilt in leaving. But I did anyway, because I loved him and I knew deep down he loved me, and that his worst fears would come true when I walked out on him. Even worse, to find out that I eventually ended up with Ben anyway would surely kill him inside.

I had made the wrong choice once already. I wasn't about to do it again. I was going to start living the life I wanted, the life I should have had from the beginning. I was done choosing the wrong man. I would grab hold of Ben and never let him go. It was my turn to shine and be loved in the way I deserved.

"I need to go, Ben," I whispered.

"Where?"

"You know where."

"Let me get dressed, and I will come with you."

I laughed. "You know that's not going to happen."

"I would stand beside you against any adversary."

I looked into his eyes and smiled. "I know you would, but this is something I need to do on my own, for me."

"I'm here if you need me. I won't leave this room until I hear from you."

I kissed him on the mouth, jumping out of bed to get dressed. I wasn't looking forward to finding Matt, but it had to be done. I said goodbye, telling him I would see him soon, and headed for the door.

CHAPTER TWENTY-ONE

Katie

I returned to our home late and was shocked to find that Matt was not there. I had assumed that was where he had gone to after he left the event, but it was clear that no one was home. Where could he have gone to? I couldn't imagine why he wouldn't return home. Though it was likely that he had gone to his office and continued to work like he always did. The team practically ran itself these days, so I couldn't imagine what he did for so many hours at the office.

I sent Ben a message letting him know that I was going to bed. I had not found Matt, and I would not be able to speak with him until the next day, and that was only if I could find him at that point. I went to find the nanny and excused her for the evening and went to check on Bella.

Bella slept soundly in her crib, not one worry in that pretty little head. The child grew more beautiful every time I saw her, if that were possible. It was the only good thing that came from my marriage, and she would never be a regret of mine. I kissed

Bella's forehead, being careful not to wake her. I returned to my own bedroom and prepared myself for bed. I was so exhausted that I fell asleep as soon as my head hit the pillow.

THE NEXT MORNING, Matt woke me up early. Confused and bleary eyed, I rolled over, unsure of where I was at first.

"Good morning, beautiful. I made you coffee."

I sat up in bed. I was irritated that Matt was waking me up so early, and I was even more irritated that he seemed in a good mood.

"Where is Bella?"

"Your parents have her. They stopped in this morning."

"Why?"

"I asked them to stop in."

I didn't like where the conversation was going. I hadn't had any coffee yet, and Matt was pretending that things were okay again. "I'm not in the mood for your plans, Matt."

"C'mon, we need to discuss last night."

I checked the clock. "What the hell, Matt. It's 7 a.m. This couldn't wait until I had a small amount of sleep or a pot of coffee?"

"I've been up all night, Katie. I can't wait any longer."

"Yes, well, where were you last night? You weren't here when I returned, and why the hell did you leave me in the first place?"

"I can't stand you being around Ben."

I rolled my eyes. "Oh for god's sake. I'm not going to be deliberately rude to someone just because you don't like him. He has done nothing wrong. You act as if he stole me away from you. I've been yours all along."

"Until last night."

"Excuse me?"

"I returned to the event to retrieve you, but you had already left."

My mouth dropped open, shocked. I took a deep breath and regained my composure. "I bet you think you're a real hero for returning after you abandoned me at a social event to find my own way home. Did you expect me to stick around and be further humiliated?"

"I'm sorry I got upset."

"That would be the understatement of the year."

"Why did you leave?"

"I didn't, not technically."

He stared at me, and I just waited him out.

"Why did you do it?" I could see in his eyes that his heart was breaking, that he knew this was the end.

"You acted like a fool, and I got tired of it."

"I think you always wanted him."

"No, that's not true. I married you because I fell in love with you."

"Then why are you leaving me?"

"I think you know why. You aren't capable of changing or letting go, and I can't spend my life arguing over the same things over and over again."

"Are you in love with him?"

"I think I've always had feelings for him, but I was in love with you and committed to our marriage. But that wasn't enough for you."

He had his head in his hands, and I knew it was all over with. I needed to start making some plans. "You need to sleep in the guesthouse, Matt. I have to be here with Bella. Until we have things figured out, you can't be in here with me."

He nodded and got up to leave the room. I took a quick shower, letting my tears flow for my failed marriage, and then called my parents to make arrangements to keep Bella for a few hours.

I needed to return to Ben and tell him that I would be his finally. I loved him and I could finally be with him forever, and I refused to wait another moment to tell him. This was my future, and I couldn't wait to start it.

SIGN UP TO RECEIVE FREE BOOKS

Sign Up to Receive Free E-Books and Audiobook Codes.

Would you like to read **The Unexpected Nanny, Dirty Little Virgin** and **other romance books** for **free**?

You can sign up to receive these free e-books and audiobooks by typing this link into your browser:

https://www.steamyromance.info/free-books-and-audiobooks-hot-and-steamy/

Or this one:

https://www.steamyromance.info/the-unexpected-nanny-free/

PREVIEW OF THE DIRTY DOCTOR'S TOUCH

A BILLIONAIRE DOCTOR ROMANCE

By Alizeh Valentine

∽

Blurb

Dirk

I am a master. An elitist. I am at the top of my field, and I know what I am doing.
Women want me. They worship me. They come to me to fulfill all their needs—all of them.
I can have any one of them I want. But I only want her.
A goddess with a perfect body. So pure, so vulnerable. She takes notice of me, but I obsess over her.
I know how this game is played, and I know she can have her pick of the lot as well. Anyone would be lucky to have her, and everyone knows it.
No matter what, no one else can have her. Everyone wants her, but only I can have her.

I will have her.
I need her.

~

Charli

I am young, strong and smart. I can make it in this world.
I know I am beautiful, and my beauty is the kind that the world finds captivating. I turn heads everywhere I go. I might not act like I notice, but I do.
Yet, life is a game. Love is a game. Beauty is a game.
I am beautiful, right?
Everyone is telling me to change. I'm not good enough as I am. I need to be better.
I want to be on top of the world, but I feel knocked to my knees.
I will rise again.

CHAPTER 1

Charli

"No, no, no! Come on, Baby, focus! Focus!"

I cringe as my Uncle Harvey walks over, his notebook tucked under his arm and a pen behind his ear. With round, mirrored sunglasses that would do John Lennon proud and a bowler cap pulled down to his eyebrows, he doesn't quite pull off the eccentric look—although he certainly is trying. Of course, no one is going to say that out loud. As one of the biggest producers in Hollywood, Harvey Sykes can look however he wants and still have the respect of everyone in the room.

"I'm sorry, can we try it again?" I ask, already knowing what he's going to say.

"We're going to have to. That was deplorable acting. I would have thought that my own flesh and blood would have it a little more together than that!" He shakes his head as he walks away, making gestures to the sound guy and the film guy.

I feel my cheeks flush red. This is the first day going through the scene, and I feel like I am the only one who is causing any kind of issues.

Here I am, trying to live my dream, and I feel like I'm floundering. There are more A-list actors present than I can count, and I can't even remember how to get a single line out of my mouth without screwing it up somehow. My uncle isn't being much help, either. I know that he is the only reason I am standing here today. I am well aware of that.

He's only reminded me thirty times. Today.

I know I shouldn't complain. It's true, he is the only reason that I've made any progress in Hollywood so far. If it weren't for Uncle Harvey, I'd be just like any other young girl from San Francisco with a dream of becoming a star on the big screen—and not having quite as much talent as I'd like to think, to back up those dreams.

"I want to take this scene from the top. Remember, Charli, never look directly into the camera. Look this way—that's right—toward the marker on the wall. We'll do the rest." He's making all kinds of gestures with his hands as he's talking, and I really am doing my best to follow along—though if I'm being completely honest, I'm not quite sure I do understand where he's telling me to look.

Of course, I'm not going to say so. I already feel like everyone else is snickering under their breath at my so-called performance, and the last thing I want to do is make it worse. Uncle Harvey thought he was doing me a favor giving me the lead role in his next big blockbuster film, but so far I feel like I am going to single-handedly tear it apart. I'm trying to get through my lines, but in the back of my mind, I can already see the headlines and the reviews.

Worst movie of the year.

Charli Sykes's career is over before it began.

Thank God for the supporting roles, the lead was a complete joke.

I try not to let my imagination get the better of me. Suddenly, I realize that it's my turn.

"I'm sorry, Jacob, but it's not working anymore. We've tried. Don't ever tell me that I didn't!" I feel proud of myself. I delivered my lines perfectly that time, and I can only imagine the congratulations my uncle is going to give me when we've finished.

"And, scene!" the director shouts.

I walk over to my uncle—no, I strut over to him, feeling more like one of the stars who are drinking mimosas on the sidelines and watching me make a complete fool out of myself.

"What did you think?" I ask coyly. He doesn't even bother to look up at me.

"Awful."

"What!"

"That was atrocious. Charli, who are you talking to? What emotions are you trying to convey? You may as well be breaking up with a jar of mayonnaise as the love of your life. That was simply awful," he shakes his head in disappointment. "And what's this?" He motions to the sweatshirt I'm wearing, and I look down self-consciously.

"It's a hoodie," I lamely remark.

"I can see that, but what in the hell are you doing wearing it here?"

"Jack said that we aren't going to be in costume until later—" I try, but he interrupts.

"I don't give a damn what Jack said. Costume or not, you're going to have to start looking the part if you are going to get into this business." He reaches forward and blatantly unzips the top of my hoodie, revealing far more cleavage than I am comfortable sharing.

"Excuse me! What do you think you're doing?" I snap.

"I'm helping you, and Baby, you need all the help you can get," he replies in an icy tone. "If you are going to be a celebrity, start looking like one."

"I don't have the figure of a celebrity!" I retort, masking the hurt in my voice.

"Not yet, but you will. Look at this and let me know what you think." He hands me a brochure for a plastic surgeon in town, and I laugh.

"What, do you want me to get a nose job?" I sneer.

"Not quite. Open it." I obey, and to my horror, I can see he's underlined the breast augmentation section.

"No!" I say, trying to hand the brochure back to him. He raises his eyebrow.

"What?"

"I'm not getting a boob job!"

"Oh, yes you are."

"Over my dead body."

"Actually, over your dead career." He pulls out the contract I signed a few days before. I have to admit, I didn't read it through as thoroughly as I should have, and my heart sinks. After opening it and flipping through a few pages, he shows me where the surgery was listed as mandatory—and where I signed that I would comply.

"I didn't know that was in there!" I try to argue, but he slips the contract back in the pages of the notebook.

"That's not my problem. If you want to star in this movie, you'll look the part. If you don't, then you'll be in breach of contract and I'll be forced to take legal action against you." He turns to go.

"You mean you'd sue your own niece?" I say, mustering as much attitude as I can. I wouldn't put it past him, but at the same time, I am going to do my best to rub in the guilt while I still can. He's used to this game, and I'm not. He knows what he's doing and he does it well.

"Well, I suppose that wouldn't look good for publicity's sake, but at the same time, neither does breaching your first contract as an actress. If you would agree to ending your acting career and going home, then I would drop the charges. But Charli, don't think you can get the best of me. I have eyes and ears everywhere." He smiles at me and I'm reminded of why my mother always called him the creepy uncle.

But, he has a point. With a sigh, I look through the brochure once more. This is what actors and actresses do. They modify themselves to look the part. I should be glad for the opportunity, he tells me.

With a sigh I finally shove the brochure in the pocket of my hoodie.

"Fine, I'll look into it." I try to be a diva, but he merely smiles.

"Excellent. Hollywood is going to look good on you."

CHAPTER 2

Charli

"All you have to do is walk in there and tell them your name, everything else is taken care of." My uncle's voice sounds more irritated than anything as it comes through my phone.

"I didn't make an appointment, though."

"Angela did it for you, just like I already told you. Your job is to show up and look the part. Agents take care of everything else." He sounds exasperated.

"I guess I'm just not used to that," I say, using my diva voice.

"Welcome to Hollywood, Baby." He hangs up the phone before I have the chance to say anything else, and I shake my head.

I love acting and living in Hollywood, but I can't say that I'm ever going to get used to this lifestyle. At least, I don't think I am. I've always been the one in charge of getting things done in my life, how am I just going to hand that responsibility over to some agent and hope they do it the right way?

Even now, as I take the elevator up to the ninth floor to the plastic surgeon's office, I'm not convinced that the receptionist is going to know who I am when I tell her my name. I walk down the long hall, following the signs on the wall rather than suffering through the embarrassment of asking for directions.

Finally, I find the right place and open the door. There are a few women seated in the waiting room, and one man. The man looks up from his magazine and eyes me as I walk in, but I ignore him. There are more aspiring actors and actresses in this town than I know what to do with. I honestly don't care what movie he's working on, or what kind of plastic surgery he needs to get the part.

I don't even want my imagination to go in that direction.

The receptionist is seated in a room behind sliding glass, and I feel awkward as I look around for a way to get her attention. She's not on the phone, but she's not looking at me, either. Shyly, I lightly tap on the glass and she turns, looking annoyed. After holding up a finger and taking her time finishing whatever it was she was doing, she slides open the glass with a rather loud bang.

"Can I help you?"

"Yes, my name is Charli Sykes, and I'm here for a consultation with Dr. Carr." I try to sound important, but she is already running her finger down a list of names on a sheet of paper. I can't help but wonder why it's not in the computer system, but I don't say anything.

"What's the consultation for?" she asks as she looks up.

"Um, plastic surgery," I say lamely.

"Of course, honey, everyone is in here for plastic surgery. I mean what kind?" She has a very rude tone to her voice, and I want to tell her to back off. But I'm already dying of embarrassment, and I don't want to make this situation any worse.

"Breast augmentation," I say in a low voice.

"Pardon?"

"Breast augmentation!" I say flatly. I can hear the sound of magazine pages rustling behind me, and can only imagine the smirks on their faces. She holds my gaze for a moment, then looks at the list.

"Oh yes, I see you're down for 1:30 PM. You've got ten minutes to wait." She points with her pen to one of the seats, and I hesitate as I look around.

"I was hoping if I arrived early I might get in a little earlier," I say, and she looks at me with a smug look on her face.

"That's not how it works here, sweetie."

I spend the ten minutes waiting with my eyes glued to the front of a cooking magazine. I'm not sure why they have this in a plastic surgery waiting room, but I guess I can't complain. At last, the nurse opens the door and calls my name, and though I refuse to look around, I can feel the stares of everyone in the waiting room.

"I see you are here for a breast augmentation consultation?" The nurse smiles and I feel somewhat more at ease.

"Yes, and I'm really not sure what to expect. Should I put on a gown?"

"No, no, not this time. He's just going to talk to you—let you know what you can expect in the procedure and the process. I'll let him know you're in here." The nurse leaves and I sit on the examination table, hoping to just get this over with.

When the door opens, I expect an old man to walk in. Instead, I look up to find the hottest man I've ever seen in my life.

"Miss Sykes? Hello, Dr. Dirk Carr. How are you?" He extends his hand and I take it, fumbling over my words.

I do my best to focus on what he is saying, but the way he smiles when he looks at me is making it difficult for me to concentrate on anything. Suddenly, I realize he's asked me a question.

"I'm sorry?"

"I asked how old you are. You seem very young, and this is quite a procedure. It's something I want all my clients to be certain of before they do." He smiles and my cheeks burn.

"I'm twenty-three." I say, feeling ashamed that I am trying to sound grown-up. I want to ask him how old he is—he looks way too young to be one of the top surgeons in this town—but he continues.

"May I see?" he asks. My smile fades.

"See?"

"Yes, your breasts. I need to know what we're starting with if I can tell you what we're going to end up with," he laughs. I awkwardly unzip my hoodie and take it off, leaving me sitting there in just my skimpy tank.

"The shirt and bra too, if you don't mind." I feel as though I'm going to pass out. Of course I mind. But I guess this is what I'm here for.

He reassures me and gives me his best doctor speech as I reluctantly pull my top off and unclasp my bra, watching his face as I pull it away. It's nearly impossible to read past the professionally vacant expression in his eyes, though I'm certain he appears to be pleased with what he sees.

"Okay, so it says here that you are hoping to go up at least two cup sizes, perhaps even three—is that correct?" I am sitting with my shirt off and my breasts hanging out. The last thing I want to talk about now is cup sizes. But, I know that he is waiting for an answer, and I nod.

"I guess. That's what my uncle told me I needed for the movie," I say.

He looks up with an amused smile. "Sounds like something he'd want."

I'm surprised. "You know who he is?"

"Harvey Sykes, the producer."

I want to know how he knows that, but he doesn't elaborate. Instead, he has me lie back on the table and lays a towel over me, finally covering my chest. Then he picks up a chart and begins to show me the different kinds of breasts. While I'm trying to focus on what he's saying and answer his questions, I just want to die.

I can't believe this gorgeous man has just seen me without my shirt on.

CHAPTER 3

Dirk

Another aspiring actress in room fourteen.

My receptionist, Angie, has seen so many of these girls walk through my doors that she doesn't bother with professionalism anymore. Not with me anyway. We often trade notes and laugh about how the appointments went afterwards. Though Angie is happily married to another woman, she still appreciates a young woman's body and wants to know every detail I can share after a new client leaves the room.

This is routine for me. Mundanely routine. I'll go in there, I'll tell her that the procedure's going to be really expensive, and she'll tell me she'll get her rich boyfriend to pay for it. Plain and simple.

I'm surprised, however, when I read the name on the chart. Charli Sykes. I've never met the girl in person, but I've seen plenty of photos of her.

Her uncle and I have worked together many times throughout the years. In fact, he's my number one referral. His clients come in all shapes and sizes, from all backgrounds, but they all only want one thing. Part of me wonders why he would send his niece in here—from the photos he's shown me she already looks like she's star material.

Another part of me is glad he did.

I go into the room and I find I'm surprised again. She's much more shy and nervous than my typical client. Usually my patients know exactly what they want and aren't shy about telling me, but there's something different about Charli.

I make small talk with her and I tell her the basics, then it comes time for the big reveal. As much as I try to be professional, a little part of me is excited as I ask her to take off her shirt and bra. Don't get me wrong, it's not her alone that I get this thrill for—I love it any time I have a star actress sitting on my table.

Of course, the more experienced actresses are more than willing to rip their top off for any guy who asks, but there's something so innocent about the newly arrived actresses who have yet to make it big. I don't see as many of the fresh-faced girls as I'd like—when you've made a name for yourself like I have, you get to work with the biggest names in the business —but it's always a treat when one of them is sitting on my table. They're not as jaded—they move slowly, they do their best to cover themselves though it's my job to look at the thing they're trying to hide. They are just so pure and untouched by fame.

For now.

Charli is no different from the rest as far as shyness goes. In fact, she might be even more shy than many of the first timers. It's clear she doesn't want to take her shirt off, and once she has it off, she doesn't want me to look at her breasts.

"Don't worry, I'm a professional, and I'm going to give you my professional opinion," I try to reassure her. But as soon as her shirt comes off, I find it incredibly difficult to be professional. For the first time in my entire career, I want nothing more than to take this young woman right here on my table.

Her breasts are perfect—her body is perfect. They are a little on the small side for Hollywood, but they are perfectly shaped and exquisitely proportioned to the rest of her body. I get to take them in my hands, but I can't fondle them like I'm dying to do.

I want to bury my face in them and breathe her in deeply. I want to lick and suck on her nipples. I want to take her so hard —but I have to hide all of these feelings and maintain a professional atmosphere. It would be a lot easier if I didn't have these beauties right there in front of my face, so, I ask her to lay back and I cover her with a towel—something I never do.

I've never reacted this way with a patient before, and I need to clear my head. I've seen more breasts than I can ever remember, so what's so different about Charli?

I can concentrate a little better with her torso covered, though it's difficult for me to go over the charts with her. Of course, I know how to mask how I'm feeling—I've done it a thousand times with other women before, hiding your thoughts and emotions is simply part of being a doctor—but this is the first time I have ever felt truly challenged in doing this. I can see Charli is doing her best to focus on the charts, but she seems distracted. I can only imagine it's because she's not used to taking off her top for strange men she's just met, and part of me is pleased.

"I just really want it to look—well, natural," she says at last.

I look down at her. Her young, beautiful face looks unsure, and I feel bad for her. Of course she wants to look natural, and I know I could do something for her that she would probably love. But, on the other hand, I'm not so sure that I want to play any part in changing her gorgeous body.

"Real natural beauty is far better than any falsely natural look in my opinion," I hear myself saying. I don't mean it as bluntly as it comes out, and she immediately looks up at me with wide eyes.

"What do you mean?"

"Well, Miss Sykes, if I'm going to be perfectly honest with you—and I am—I don't know why your uncle wants you to get this done. Your body is perfect just as it is." I smile as I speak, and I can see by the look in her eyes she doesn't believe me. However, her face flushes a deep, crimson red and I know I've flattered her.

"He says every woman in Hollywood has breasts like those." She points to one of the models on the chart I was showing her, and I shake my head.

"There are plenty of successful actresses who have smaller breasts. Look, I'm not trying to talk you out of this, I just want you to be sure that it's what you want before you go through with it." I smile and she looks away.

It's clear that she is torn about something, and I would do anything to help her. She suddenly looks up at me.

"If I were to go through with it, what would the cost be to go up two sizes?" I feel my heart sink a bit. I don't know what's wrong with me—here is a client coming from one of the wealthiest producers in Hollywood. I could quote her whatever I liked and he would be more than happy to pay, knowing that I'd produce a work of art that would turn heads everywhere she went from here on out.

But then, I don't really want to do the surgery. I don't want this girl to make herself look fake because her uncle thinks she should. I want to show her what it's like to be appreciated for who she is—just how she is. She's perfect. I reluctantly pick up another book and flip it open, naming her several quotes. I can't help but smile when her eyes widen.

"Your uncle is going to pay for this, I assume?" I ask with a grin. She nods, though she is still white as a sheet.

"Good. Well, think it over and let me know what you decide. Let your uncle know that I cut him a good deal on this, too. I've recently raised my personal fee for such surgeries, and that alone adds several thousand dollars to the cost." I smile once more, and she shakes her head. Suddenly, I realize she is still lying on the table under the towel, and for the first time in as long as I can remember, I feel slightly embarrassed.

"You can get dressed," I tell her—though I would much rather stand there and stare at her perfect body all day.

CHAPTER 4

Charli

I grab my tank and yank it over my head, embarrassed that I'd chosen such a skimpy top to wear. Of course I wore the hoodie over the top, but what must he think of me? Does he think that I normally run about with practically nothing on? Then again, this is Hollywood, and I haven't exactly seen a lot of people concerned about the amount of skin they show in public.

"I hope that I was able to answer all your questions," he says as he watches me put my clothing back on. I refuse to make eye contact with him as I zip up my hoodie once more—zipping it up high enough to hide any cleavage my bra created. There's a part of me that thinks he is almost disappointed that I covered so much of myself, but then, I refuse to let myself think about that.

"Yes, thank you. I think that should be all that he needs to know," I say. I still feel awkward discussing the size of my breasts with anyone, let alone my uncle or this gorgeous man in front of me, but I have no choice.

"Here, let me write a few things down for you that you can

pass along. That way you'll be certain to remember everything." Dr. Carr smiles as he scribbles a few things down on a piece of paper in his notebook. He tears the page free and hands it to me, then he hands me a few more brochures.

"Just so you know for sure what you are going to be facing as far as aftercare goes. I know it can be difficult when you are in the middle of a project, and he might want you to get it done as soon as possible. Although once again I can't help but say I don't think this procedure is necessary for you. You're perfect." Dr. Carr clasps his hands behind his back and I blush despite my biggest efforts not to.

"Thank you," I say again. I don't know what else to say. The most attractive man I have ever seen in my life just told me that I have a perfect body—how would any girl respond to that?

I can't help but be a little confused by his assessment. Why would he tell me something that would lose him money? Was he giving me his professional opinion—it's his job to recognize beauty, after all—or was he being a little more personal?

He opens the door and points me down the hall, and I give him a small wave as I leave.

I can't get him out of my mind the entire drive back to my apartment. I know I have to get down to the studio and meet with my uncle, but I'm going to take a minute to change into something a little less revealing first.

His black hair. His dark blue eyes. I think I might have even detected the bottom part of a tattoo when he rolled up his sleeves to examine me.

To examine me! The memory of that man with my breasts cupped in his hands is almost more than I can bear. I can feel a heat in my loins as I drive and I shake my head.

I've only ever been with one other man in my life—and he could hardly be considered a man. My boyfriend and I had slept together on prom night, and I had to admit, it was a huge letdown. I tried to excuse it as us both being eighteen and not knowing what we were doing, but ever since that night I've never really wanted to have sex with anyone in else. It just didn't seem exciting after my disappointing experience.

I was too busy with my acting career to worry about boys in college, and now here I am, dreaming about the man who has given me a breast exam for surgery. Maybe it's time for me to reassess my celibate lifestyle. I shake my head, clearing my thoughts of the doctor.

I have to find my uncle.

"And this is everything?"

"That's everything he gave me besides this bit of advice. He doesn't think I should go through with the surgery."

"What? Why?" Uncle Harvey looks at me with raised eyebrows. I can't tell if there is concern in his eyes or not, but I continue anyway.

"He says my body is perfect just the way I am. He doesn't think that I need surgery to fix anything." I smirk, but it fades when my uncle bursts into laughter.

"Well, that's why he's in that line of work, and I'm in this one. Excellent. I want you to give them a call and set an appointment right away. During recovery we can film some of the slower scenes. And you can use that time to work on your lines." He beams as he turns on his heel and walks away, but I can't help but call after him.

"I don't think I really need to—"

"Remember the contract!" he shouts back. I sigh. There is no winning.

I wait until the next day to call.

The phone rings and rings, and I can't help but think that the receptionist is sitting there, letting it ring off the hook as she stares blankly at the computer screen in front of her. When the answering machine picks up, I am tempted just to hang up and try again later.

On impulse, I decide to leave a message.

"This is Charli Sykes. I wanted to set an appointment for surgery, so if you could give me a call back as soon as you get this, I would very much appreciate it." I leave my number and hang up, skeptical that the receptionist will ever call me back—she didn't seem to be too fond of me when I was in the office. Now, it's time to focus on the rest of the day.

It's not until late in the afternoon when my phone finally rings. I look down, and not recognizing the number, answer. I'm surprised to hear Dr. Carr's voice on the other end of the line.

"Hey, I got your message and was just giving you a call back," he says.

"I thought that's what you have a receptionist for." Why am I teasing him?

"She's out at lunch, and I didn't want to leave you hanging. Anyway, there are a few more things I would like to discuss with you before we go ahead and set the date for the surgery, but I would prefer to discuss it over lunch rather than in the office." He speaks casually, but my guard is up.

"Lunch?" I ask. It's seems kind of strange for a plastic surgeon to discuss a procedure over lunch, but maybe that's just the way people do things in this town.

"Sure, no doubt you'll want to get away from all the stress of the set for an hour or two. Besides, you're technically going to still be working." He laughs at his little joke and I can't help but smile in spite of myself. It wasn't a date, after all, but I could always pretend.

"How about going down to Starsky's?" he asks and I almost drop my phone. That is a five star restaurant, and one of the most expensive ones in town at that. My lunch alone would cost me a week's salary. I hesitate, not knowing how to answer.

"This is a client lunch, so I'll pick up the tab," he prompts. That is an offer I can't refuse, and though I feel strange doing it, I hear myself accepting his invitation.

"Excellent. Then I will see you tomorrow at one if that works for you?"

"One o'clock works fine for me. See you then, and thank you." I hang up the phone, ignoring the flutter in my stomach. I'll probably never get used to the way they do things around here.

If you want to continue reading this story, you can get your copy from your favorite vendor by searching for the title:

The Dirty Doctor's Touch
A Billionaire Doctor Romance

You can also find the e-book version by typing this link in your computer's browser:

https://www.hotandsteamyromance.com/products/the-dirty-doctor-s-touch-a-billionaire-doctor-romance

OTHER BOOKS BY THIS AUTHOR

Saving Her Rescuer: A Billionaire & A Virgin Romance

I was just trying to get away from my crazy ex for the weekend when I ended up in a giant pileup on the highway up to Gore Mountain.

https://geni.us/SavingHerRescuer

∼

Sensual Sounds: A Rockstar Ménage

Lust. Lies. Double lives.

The rock and roll industry is full of people who are looking out for themselves and willing to do anything to rise to the top.

https://www.hotandsteamyromance.com/collections/frontpage/products/sensual-sounds-a-rockstar-menage

∼

On the Run: A Secret Baby Romance

Murder. Lies. Fraud. Just another day in the lives of billionaires and women on the run.

https://www.hotandsteamyromance.com/collections/frontpage/products/on-the-run-a-secret-baby-romance

∼

The Dirty Doctor's Touch: A Billionaire Doctor Romance

I am a master. An elitist. I am at the top of my field, and I know what I am doing.

https://www.hotandsteamyromance.com/collections/frontpage/products/the-dirty-doctor-s-touch-a-billionaire-doctor-romance

---

The Hero She Needs: A Single Daddy Next Door Romance

He's the only man I've ever wanted...

https://www.hotandsteamyromance.com/collections/frontpage/products/the-hero-she-needs-a-single-daddy-next-door-romance

---

You can find all of my books here

Hot and Steamy Romance

https://www.hotandsteamyromance.com

Facebook

facebook.com/HotAndSteamyRomance

COPYRIGHT

©Copyright 2020 by Scarlett King - All rights Reserved

In no way is it legal to reproduce, duplicate, or transmit any part of this document in either electronic means or in printed format. Recording of this publication is strictly prohibited and any storage of this document is not allowed unless with written permission from the publisher. All rights are reserved.

Respective authors own all copyrights not held by the publisher.

www.ingramcontent.com/pod-product-compliance
Lightning Source LLC
LaVergne TN
LVHW021710060526
838200LV00050B/2592